JILLIAN HART

grew up on her family's homestead, where she helped raise cattle, rode horses and scribbled stories in her spare time. After earning her English degree from Whitman College, she worked in travel and advertising before selling her first novel. When Jillian isn't working on her next story, she can be found puttering in her rose garden, curled up with a good book or spending quiet evenings at home with her family.

JANET TRONSTAD

grew up on a farm in central Montana, spending many winter days reading books. None of those books were as eagerly consumed as the ones about Christmas though. Stars. Sleighs. The story of the Christ Child being born. She loved them all. That's why, almost every year since she started writing the Dry Creek series, there's a new Christmas book. Janet lives in Pasadena, California, where she is a full-time writer.

Mail-Order Christmas Brides

JILLIAN HART

JANET TRONSTAD

Love Inspired

Recycling programs
for this product may
not exist in your area.

LOVE INSPIRED BOOKS

ISBN-13: 978-0-373-82895-1

MAIL-ORDER CHRISTMAS BRIDES

Copyright © 2011 by Harlequin Books S.A.

The publisher acknowledges the copyright holders
of the individual works as follows:

HER CHRISTMAS FAMILY
Copyright © 2011 by Jill Strickler

CHRISTMAS STARS FOR DRY CREEK
Copyright © 2011 by Janet Tronstad

www.LoveInspiredBooks.com

Printed in U.S.A.

CONTENTS

HER CHRISTMAS FAMILY

Jillian Hart

That their hearts may be encouraged,
being knit together in love.
—*Colossians* 2:2

Chapter One

Montana Territory, December 1884

Tate Winters tipped the brim of his Stetson to cut the glare of the sun, watching as the westbound train squealed to a noisy stop along the depot's platform. The great metal beast spewed steam, smoke and uniformed men who ran to set brakes, open doors and toss out luggage. He braced his shoulders, preparing for the worst.

Who knew what sort of woman was going to step off that train? She could be homely, she could be desperate, she could be so bitter and sharp-tongued that no man who'd ever met her would have her. The way he saw it, he had to be ready for just about any type of horror a woman could bring a man.

"Pa, do you see her?" Gertie clutched his hand, her fingers so small and slight within his own. "Do you see my new ma?"

"Hard to say, since I don't know what she looks

like." He didn't care how ugly the woman was. He'd promised to marry her and he would. His life might be in shambles and there wasn't a thing of his heart left, but he hadn't been able to say no to his daughter's wish. Gertie, eight years old, wanted a mother. After everything she had lost, everything his mistakes had cost her, he could not deny her the one thing she wanted most. Regardless of how disagreeable, quarrelsome or shrewish Miss Felicity Sawyer was, as long as she would devote herself to his little girl, he would put a ring on her finger.

"Ooh, look at the pretty lady." Gertie breathed the words in awe and jabbed one finger. "Is that her?"

Tate took in the cheerful woman in a bright yellow dress with a daisy—yes, a daisy—mounted on her bonnet. What kind of woman wore a hat like that in winter? Slender, graceful, lovely. No way would such a beauty need to resort to answering a marriage advertisement in the territorial newspaper. No way would that woman be desperate enough to marry a stranger.

"She's like a princess." Gertie looked captivated, blue eyes wide, button face hopeful. "Like some of the stories in my books, Pa."

"She isn't for us. Let's find the woman who is." He leaned heavily on his cane and took a careful step. The pain wasn't as bad these days but it was still enough to make him grit down on his molars when he transferred weight onto his left leg. He ignored the glance of disdain a few townswomen threw his way as they bustled by. He'd gotten used to that pain, too.

"But, Pa, the pretty lady is all alone." Gertie went

up on tiptoe straining to see through the milling crowd. "No one's comin' to greet her."

"I told you. Leave it be. She's not who we're looking for." Relief shot through him when he spotted a squat, rotund looking woman with a pointy nose and an unhappy pinch to her rather homely face. "There she is. That's your Miss Sawyer."

"I don't think so." Curls bounced as she shook her head. "Felicity said in her letters she had blond hair just like me. That lady there has brown hair. She can't be my new ma."

He knew what it was like, that sinking feeling of realizing what you got in life was far short of what you wanted. He hated that his daughter might be disappointed, but hadn't he warned her? Hadn't he tried to keep her from getting her hopes set too high?

"The brown-haired lady looks mighty sensible to me." He limped forward, shoulders straight, trying not to look like the cripple that injustice had made him. "That's what a little girl needs in a mother. Someone practical, someone who knows what life is about. You go on up to meet her now."

"Pa, I told you. It's not her. Look."

Sure enough, some tall, rail-thin fellow strolled up to the stout woman and offered her his arm. With contented smiles, the pair whisked off, leaving him gaping in shock like a fish out of water. Fine, so that wasn't his bride. Miss Sawyer had to be around here somewhere. "Best check toward the other end of the train."

"Pa, the pretty lady is just standing by herself. No one has come for her." Excitement rang like music in his daughter's voice. She tugged his hand, holding on so hard. He could feel her hopes rising, soaring like prayers toward the sky. He grimaced, wondering what was best to say to keep her from getting hurt.

Up ahead the beautiful lady had her back to them, exchanging words with a baggage handler. A battered-looking trunk stood between them. Her melodious "thank you" lifted into the air as sweetly as church music.

He'd given up on God, but if he still thought the Lord listened, then he would have asked for help for his Gertie. The crowd surrounding them was thinning, save for a few farewell wishers waving to loved ones who had just boarded the train. Doors closed, men called out, the engine idled harder until the entire train shook like a wild animal about to bolt.

No other woman was left on the platform. Miss Sawyer was a no-show. She had changed her mind without sending word and abandoned Gertie. The girl was going to be shattered.

"C'mon." No tender notes sounded in his voice. He had no tenderness left to give. Couldn't remember the last time he did. He wished he had some, even the smallest trace, so he could offer it as comfort to his daughter. "She didn't show."

"No. Felicity wouldn't leave me."

"Let's head home." He knew about being stubborn, about wanting something so badly you couldn't let go of it even when all chance was gone. "No tears now. You got your hopes up too high."

"I know, Pa." Her chin sank down and she gave

a little sniff. Her hand tucked in his went slack. Her shoes dragged along the platform.

Blast that Sawyer woman. His cane thumped loudly on the platform. Anger licked through him. He should have figured this would happen. Women didn't keep promises, and if they did it was only because it was to their benefit. His girl didn't deserve this, she'd had too many disappointments in her short life.

"Gertie?" A woman's voice called out, a sweet melodic sound. "Is that you?"

"Felicity?" The child spun around so fast, he lost his balance. Her hand slipped out of his, leaving him lurching against his cane as she took off at a dead run toward the smiling blonde. "I knew you would come. I *knew* it."

"I would never break a promise to you, my very own little girl." To his horror the stunning woman opened her arms wide to wrap his daughter in a motherly hug, the silk daisy on her hat bobbing.

That woman was Miss Sawyer? She was going to be his new wife? His knees buckled. Air whooshed out of his lungs. His heart forgot to beat, of course there were some who said he didn't have a heart. He blinked, but the woman was still there, bending down to chatter excitedly with Gertie.

He swallowed hard, nearly choking. What cruel joke was this? He shook his head, not wanting to believe what was right before his eyes. He squinted, looking at the woman, really looking at her. She was gorgeous—slender and petite, her locks of gold done up just so, her face as finely carved as a china doll's.

Big blueberry eyes, a rosebud mouth and the daintiest chin he'd ever seen made him blow out a breath and stumble forward.

This simply couldn't be right. His cane's grip felt numb in his hand. All of him felt numb. Every step he took brought him closer to her. Easier to see the details now, the sunny smile, the pearls at her collar, the life sparkling out of her. She wasn't what he'd bargained for, not even close to what he wanted. She was not going to fit into his life. She was not going to work into his plans. She was going to have to turn around, climb aboard that train and go anywhere, somewhere else, even back where she came from. She wasn't going to stay with him.

"Felicity, you've gotta meet Pa." Gertie dragged the woman by one hand in his direction. "He's a real good pa, especially now that we're back together again."

Too late to head the other way. Hiking off into the mountains and staying put sounded like a good option. Too late to figure out a way to get her back on the train. The great iron beast roared, the whistle blew and the contraption took off, shaking the platform like a blizzard hitting. At least the train's departure postponed the moment when he had to exchange pleasantries with the woman.

He kept his eyes glued to the boards at his feet, letting her get a good long look at him. Let her see the cane. Let her see the failure he wore like a shabby coat, notice he wasn't wearing a wealthy man's duds. He was a simple working man, these days not doing much better than living paycheck to paycheck. Reckoned she was wishing herself back on that train about now, realizing that his best days were behind him. He'd been forced to settle for a mail-order wife because no one who knew him would have him.

"Tate?" Warmth softened her dulcet alto, tempting him to look up and meet her gaze, but he had to resist. He squared his shoulders, drew himself up straight and clamped his jaw tight. Prepared, her disappointment in him would hurt less.

"It's awkward, isn't it?" She rustled closer, fine shoes tapping on the plank platform, her hand tucked tightly around Gertie's. "What do you say to a stranger you are about to marry? I've pondered it the entire trip and I just could never think of the exact right thing."

"Me, neither." The words came out gruffly. He shifted his cane as if he didn't know what to say next.

"I figured you for the shy sort, since you let Gertie answer my first letter." She stopped before him, petticoats swishing. A cold wind gusted hard, blowing a piece of rattling paper across the platform like a leaf in the wind, and she shivered. "My youngest sister was shy, too, so I understand completely. I will try not to be too exuberant. It's a fault of mine."

"I see." He didn't so much as blink his long dark eyelashes. Tate Winters wasn't at all what she'd imagined from Gertie's written descriptions of her beloved pa. Like those descriptions, he was tall. He did have dark blue eyes, but that was where the similarities ended. This man walked with a cane. This man's gaze looked shadowed and full of pain.

"That's your trunk?" His baritone was colder than

the gusts knocking her back a step. He still hadn't looked at her.

"Yes. Just the one." She pitched her voice, turning toward him, willing him to see her. Didn't he like her? Couldn't he at least be polite? A terrible foreboding gripped her stomach. Had she made a mistake in coming? Had she chosen the wrong man?

As he lumbered by, all six feet plus of him, she remembered the exact moment she'd decided to answer his advertisement. *Wife needed,* she read on that crisp September morning, skimming the ads as she always did while sipping coffee. The clatter of steel forks on ironware rang around her in the dining room of the Iowa boardinghouse where she'd lived. She had bent closer, interested enough to keep reading. *All I want is someone to be kindly to my daughter,* he'd written. *Little Gertrude deserves a good ma.*

Her imagination had taken off at those words. She'd set her cup into its saucer, stared out the window where clothes slapped on a line, where her life was a string of long lonely days, and pictured a father who loved his little girl so much, he put concern for her first.

Wasn't that heartening? Time had robbed her of all but a few memories of her father, but the impact of his kindness remained. Smallpox had taken her parents when she was young.

As she watched the man with the bitter expression grab a handle on the end of her trunk and heft it onto one brawny shoulder, she forced herself to remember his advertisement. When she read his simple request, she had instantly come to care about him, a perfect stranger, hundreds of miles away. Her trunk might be heavy but he handled it as if it were weightless, balancing its bulk with his free hand. He was a strong man, powerfully built, handsome when he took an awkward step and the sunshine touched his face. Strong bones, straight nose, a generous mouth that may have once smiled.

His gaze, when it finally swept over her, was hard as stone and hit her like a punch. It wasn't dislike of her, but desolation she saw. The smothering, human pain of someone who had lost all hope. Bleak despair echoed in the depths of his eyes and turned her to ice before he swung away.

That was when she noticed the fraying sleeves of his coat, in want of mending. A small tear near the hem of his faded denims. He wore no muffler or gloves on this frigid December day, nor did Gertie, whose hand felt fragile cradled in her own.

Hardship was everywhere. It had ruined her family, taken her parents and separated her from her sisters. How close had hardship come to destroying this family? She gazed down into the girl's face and into eyes full of silent need. It had been a lifetime since someone had held on to her this tight or wanted her as desperately.

Felicity thought of the letter tucked inside her reticule, written in Gertie's careful print. *Please be my ma for Christmas. I promise to be really good if only you will come.*

Love at first word, that's what this was, the deep

abiding tie that had instantly bound her spirit to the girl's only strengthened. She knew what it was like to ache after a mother who was gone and to long for a mother yet to be. Too many years she'd been a little girl standing in the yard waiting hopefully whenever a married couple came to choose among the orphans. She'd prayed with all the power of her soul to be the one selected. She'd been passed by every time.

Gertie seemed to sense something was wrong. Tears brimmed, one after another. "You're gonna stay, aren't you, Felicity?"

"Wild horses couldn't pry me away." She saw herself in Gertie's eyes, longing to be loved. She brushed at the girl's tears with the pad of her thumb, already a mother to this child. The wedding ceremony was merely a technicality. "Let's go catch up with your pa. Take me home, Gertie."

Chapter Two

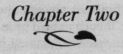

This was a disaster of epic proportion. Tate ground down the depot steps, aware of the tap of a woman's shoes directly behind him. The whisper of her petticoats, the rustle of her skirt, the low melody of her voice as she chatted with Gertie grated, and he clamped his jaw tight. He closed his ears to the sound of that pleasing tone. Best not to listen to a thing she said. Best not to get attached because the woman wasn't staying.

He heaved the trunk onto the wagon bed, wondering what frills and foppery the woman had brought with her. Fancy women like that liked fine frocks. No doubt her hands beneath her gloves were soft and smooth, never having known a day's work. He grimaced as he latched the tailgate, the chain chattering in the cold. He shook his head. No, he could not imagine the woman who swept into sight was any happier with this situation than he was. Once she saw there was no maid to wait on her, no housekeeper to order about, she would race for the next train out of town so fast she'd be a blur dashing down the platform. No doubt about that. He squared his shoulders and steeled his chest, his only defense against her nearness.

"Pa, guess what?" Gertie stumbled up to him, nearly tripping with her excitement. He couldn't remember the last time her big blue eyes had sparkled like that, nor the last time he'd seen her dear smile framed by twin dimples. Something in the vicinity of his heart caught, a muscle spasm of sorrow.

"Felicity brought me a surprise!" The wind rustled the ends of her curls and brushed the stray flyaway strands against the side of her apple cheeks as if with a loving hand. "A present. And it's not even Christmas yet."

"Huh." He kept his gaze low as he grabbed hold of his cane and ambled around the side of the wagon. The yellow ruffle of the woman's skirt stayed in his peripheral vision, following him. Whatever was going to happen to Gertie when the fancy lady took off, he didn't know. Her heart would be shattered, those sky-high hopes grounded.

Helplessness twisted inside him and wrung him out. He should have put his foot down at the depot. He should have refused the woman, ordered her back onto the train before it departed, pushed her away before she had a chance to win his daughter's heart. Look how the girl was already captured, one small hand clinging so hard to the woman's fine-knit glove it was a wonder she wasn't causing a bruise.

"She has one for you, too." Gertie bounced in place,

as if her happiness was so great not even gravity could hold her. A silent question shone in her blue eyes as she searched his. "Aren't you glad she's finally here?"

"Settle down now." He could feel the rigid lines digging into his face and the harsh set of his mouth, grown hard with hardship and defeat. Life was a grim place, but he read his daughter's anxiety as easily as if her concerns had been scribbled in ink across her forehead. His darling girl. For her sake, he tried to soften the harsh set of his face, tried to ease the hard lines around his mouth. "Get on up into the wagon."

"Yes, Pa." It was a struggle for her to find the will to let go of the woman's hand. He didn't look directly at the female. The slash of yellow hem beneath her navy coat and the beige of her wool gloves was all he cared to see of her. He could feel the weight of her gaze as he swung his child into the air and onto the wagon seat.

"Your turn." He held out one hand, making himself like iron, a cold and unfeeling thing that cannot be hurt. To his surprise, her glove lighted on his palm as gently as a bird landing, accepting his help as she placed one dainty shoe on the running board and rose up into the sun. That's how it looked when he gazed up at her with the rays of sunlight spearing down around her and her bonnet glowing.

Air froze in his lungs as he stood there, momentarily paralyzed by the sight. He'd never seen anything as beautiful as Miss Sawyer with December sunshine kissing her cheek and shimmering in her hair.

"Oh, I love your horse." She bobbed out of the sun

and settled onto the seat, still carrying wisps and glimmers of the light in her golden hair and on the silken petals of the daisy. "What is his name?"

He made the mistake of forgetting to look away. Sparkling blue eyes latched on his, holding him prisoner and stealing his every thought. He felt his jaw move and his tongue tried to form words that did not come. Confusion curled through him. Kindness curved in the upturned corners of her smile and sang in her gentle voice. He was not prepared for kindness.

"Patches," Gertie answered, her optimism ringing like church bells. The wind rose, tearing at her words and snatching them apart as he shuffled around the back of the wagon, escaping the woman's attention.

Ice slipped beneath his cane as he waited for a teamster's wagon to lumber by before stepping into the road. Gertie's conversation rose and fell in snatches, explaining about how they bought the old gelding at auction, walking between the aisles of horses until they found the very best one.

The cheapest one fit to do work, but he didn't correct her as he swung onto the seat and gathered the reins. He couldn't feel the thick leather straps against the palms of his hands. He couldn't feel anything at all as the black-and-white pinto pulled them forward into the road.

"I've always wanted a horse," the woman explained as the runners beneath the wagon box jostled over ruts in the snowy street. "My father trained horses when I was a little girl."

"When you were my age?" Gertie asked.

"I was a year younger." She gave a decisive nod and the flower on her hat nodded, too. "I remember sneaking into the stables to watch my pa with the horses. He had a voice so benevolent that every living creature leaned in closer just to hear him. I would watch, keeping as quiet as I could until the straw crinkled and he would discover me. I was supposed to be in big trouble, I was too little to be in the barn by myself, but he would always scoop me up and hold me close and let me sit on one of the horses."

"Then he died?" Gertie's chin wobbled.

"Yes. My mother, too." She smoothed away a strand of the girl's flyaway hair. "I don't know what happened to the horses. Probably whoever bought the farm kept them. I haven't had a horse since."

Don't get caught up in her sob story, he told himself as he gave the slack reins a small tug as the intersection approached. That was the way a woman hoodwinked you. They played with a man's heartstrings, tugging his emotions this way and that until they had you right where they wanted you. He glanced both ways down Main before giving the right rein a tight tug. With a face like hers, Miss Sawyer was probably used to playing men right and left. A smart man would keep that in mind when dealing with her.

"Then Patches can be part yours, too." Gertie leaned closer to the woman, absolute adoration written on her dear face.

His chest cinched tight. What was he going to do about that? Tension licked through him, more regret than anger. Why couldn't that woman be what he'd bargained for? His little girl was seriously smitten with the woman. How did he protect her from more heartache? He shook his head, not liking the situation. Not one bit. Best to do what had to be done now and get it over with. He reined Patches toward the nearest hitching post.

"Oh, this is a lovely town. Just like something out of a storybook." The woman clasped her hands, gasping with a sweet little sound that seemed genuine, not fake. He drew the gelding to a stop, his gaze arrowing to her instead of his driving. The brisk air had painted her cheeks a rosy pink, the color accentuating the fine lines of her high cheekbones and the heart shape of her dainty chin.

"The shops are decorated for Christmas. Look at the candles. This is exactly the sort of town I've always wanted to live in. It's homey and sweet and safe feeling." Sincerity rang in her words as she gazed up and down the street. "It looks as if fairy tales can happen here."

"I go to school right over there." Gertie pointed across the street, where the tailor shop hid the schoolhouse two blocks away. "I got a perfect mark in spelling today. I studied real well."

"I'm so proud of you." The woman turned her attention to his child. He didn't want to believe the tenderness he saw on her face or heard in her words as she pulled off her gloves. "I knew from your first letter you were a very smart girl."

"You did?" Gertie perked up like a dying plant

finally set in the sun. "I worked really hard on that letter."

"I could tell." She slipped one glove onto Gertie's hand. "You spelled every word perfectly. It was a very good letter."

Gertie beamed. Life came into her, something he hadn't seen since Lolly's death. His dislike of the woman fizzled as she snuggled the second glove into place and patted the girl's covered hands. "There. That ought to keep you toasty warm."

"They are so soft." Gertie held out her hands and inspected the gloves.

"I'll knit you a pair, how's that?"

Already the woman made promises to his daughter, ones she couldn't possibly keep, and that would be his fault. But someone had to put a stop to this before more damage could be done. He hopped out of the wagon. "I'll get your trunk, Miss Sawyer. Plans have changed."

"Changed?" Confused, she blinked those long curly lashes of hers. The wind played with fine gold strands of hair fallen down from the confines of her hat. "This is a hotel. I don't understand. You were going to take me to your house."

"True, but I've had second thoughts and I'm sorry about it." He braced himself for the emotional battle, often a woman's way of controlling a man. He focused on the snow compacted beneath his boots and the rhythm of his cane tapping on it. "You won't be staying with us. I'll get you a return ticket in the morning."

"What? You're sending me back?" The words rang

hollow, vibrating like a plucked string, full of pain. "I don't understand. We had an agreement."

"We did. Believe me, I wish I could keep it." He leaned his cane against his hip to wrestle with the tailgate. It killed him to admit it. "I'm sorry you came all this way, but you aren't going to fit in here. You don't suit. Surely you can feel it, too?"

"Papa! What do you mean? No. Don't send her away." Gertie's face crumpled. Life drained from her like sun from the sky. Misery said what she could not. She turned around, climbing onto her knees, gripping the seat back with Miss Sawyer's gloves still on her hands. Her blue gaze lassoed him, letting him feel her anguish.

He blinked hard against the stab of pain in his chest. He didn't want his girl hurt. That's why he was doing this. It was the right thing. That didn't give him comfort as he unwound the chain, the rattle of metal echoing straight through him as if nothing, not even his soul, remained.

"It's the best thing to do, Gertie." He tried to comfort her with his voice. "You'll never know how sorry I am."

"Oh, Papa." The springs creaked as she sat down proper and buried her face in her hands.

He broke right along with her. He had no idea how to fix the situation and scowled at the woman responsible. Miss Sawyer in her tailored clothes tapped rapidly in his direction. Already folks on the boardwalk were passing by, throwing curious glances their way. One word from any of them about his past, and she would be gone, anyway. She had options. He did not. He dropped the chain on the wagon box and reached for the trunk. A yellow ruffle flounced into view.

"How don't I suit?" Not a demand, but a plea. "You don't know me. You've hardly said a few dozen words to me."

"I just know. Isn't it obvious to you?" He couldn't be what she'd been wishing for. He dragged the trunk closer. He meant to be kind. He wished he could be. "Look, I'm not the right sort of husband for you. I'm going to do the best thing for both of us. It's better you go now than later. Better for her."

"For Gertie?" Confusion knelled in her words, drawing him closer, making him look. In the thinning afternoon light, the sun continued to find her, to glow in the golden wisps of her hair, to make luminous her ivory complexion. "I wouldn't hurt her for the world. I don't understand this."

"I'm being honest and doing what's right, Miss Sawyer—"

"Felicity," she insisted, moving in to lay her hand on his. The shock of her touch, warm and innocent on his cold skin, made his mind empty, his knees buckle and his anger fade.

The anger was just a defense. He really didn't dislike her. That was the worst part. Of all the things she could have said, he wasn't prepared for her concern toward his daughter.

"Give me a chance, that's all I'm asking." Her eyes were darker than blueberries. He could see the shadows in them, the wounds of spirit that made the muscle in his chest clamp harder. As if she sensed his weakness, she pleaded on, "At least wait until you know me before you send me away."

"What about Gertie? She wants you to stay, but you could have anyone. You are beautiful——" Heat stained his face. Bashful from fear of revealing too much, he stared hard at the square of snow visible between his boots.

"You think I'm beautiful?" She breathed the words like wonder, but surely he was only imagining that. Women like Miss Sawyer probably heard that all the time. Her hand remained on his, never moving.

What did he say? Pride held him up as he stared at the hand on his, small and delicate. The slightly rough calluses on the pads of her fingers surprised him. Up close he could see the loneliness shining in her eyes and the set of her delicate jaw, strong, as if used to facing hardship.

Now that he took the time to see it, she wore the air of a woman who'd been on her own too long and struggled to make ends meet. He finally noticed the wear on her coat, although lovingly cared for, and not the new garment he'd mistaken it to be.

"Miss, you don't look desperate enough to settle for the likes of me." He might as well admit the truth.

The truth had a startling effect on her. He watched amazed as her guard went down, as the pools that were her eyes deepened to show more of her. He looked into that well of sadness and loss, and felt the muscles where his heart used to be whip tight. He'd been so wrapped up in his own challenges, fighting to right what was wrong in his life to make things better for his daughter that he'd forgotten adversity could fall like rain, striking many people.

"You were not what I envisioned, Tate. I can't deny it." The pearls of her teeth dug into her bottom lip as she hesitated, perhaps debating the right words. "I imagined you any number of ways. Tall or short. Bony or beefy. Disagreeable or pleasant. But any way I pictured you, I prayed that what I felt when I read your advertisement was true. That you were a man who loved his daughter above all else, a man of heart and gentleness."

Her words struck like bullets in the empty place between his ribs. He cast a glance at Gertie, still bent forward on the seat, her back to him, her thin shoulders shaking with silent sobs. He wished he could turn back time, reassemble the man he used to be so he could give her the kindness she deserved.

But not even God could change the past, so he straightened his spine. He may be many things, but a coward wasn't one of them. "I am not gentle. I have no heart. And likely when you hear what folks say about me, you will be off to seek out the next man on your list who is looking for a wife."

"No. There are no others on my list. I wanted Gertie from the start. From the moment I read your words in the paper I wanted to be her mother." She changed before his eyes, drawing herself up like a woman weary of fighting battles and resigned to fight one more. Hurt etched in her fine-boned features as she set her chin another notch higher. "Tell me this one thing, it's all that I care about. Have you ever harmed a woman? Will you harm me?"

"Never. But why on earth would you want me?" Glimmers of the past flashed into his mind, memories he would not allow to take hold. He stared at the hotel's sign, debating what to do. Black letters on brass glinted in the waning sun, perhaps a sign he should not relent. He should stick to his decision and send her away. He hated how hard Gertie was crying. What should he do? "The way I see it, you've got to be hiding something. What is it, Miss Sawyer? If you are not desperate or in sad straits, then there is some other reason you're here."

"I never said I wasn't in desperate straits." Her hand on his remained, a physical link between them, and suddenly it became more. Her touch sank down as if trying to snare his emotions, somehow a bond between them.

"I lost my job as a seamstress. The town I grew up in began to die when the railroad bypassed it. First, a few businesses closed and left. Then the mill shut down. Jobs dried up. I didn't want to leave, hoping my sisters whom I was separated from would return. How else could we find each other again? So I stayed longer than I should have, living on hope and my savings until even that was gone." The fading light framed her, as if it hated to let go of such honesty.

He knew how the light felt, as he reluctantly slipped his hand from beneath hers, breaking the connection between them and any bond she tried to create. A tie that could never be. He hardened himself to it and swallowed hard.

Don't let her story soften you, he told himself, but less bitterness soured him as he checked on his daughter. Still silently crying, shaking with sobs of loss. How could he leave her sitting there like that? Worse, how could he trust her with a woman who didn't need her enough?

"I have nowhere to go, no prospects, no other advertisements I've answered. I love your daughter, Tate. I haven't had a family since I was seven years old. I can understand what Gertie has been through. I can love her better than any other woman. Just give me the chance." She glanced at the hotel sign, the tears in her eyes pooling, threatening to fall. She did not use tears to sway him, only her love that lit her like candlelight on a dark night, that warmed her like fire crackling in a home's hearth. When her gaze found his daughter, longing shone within her. He could see a mother's love as she ached for the crying girl.

"I'm not sure I can leave her. Please, don't make me." She whispered the words but they seemed to fill up the street, silencing the noise and chasing away the setting sun. Rosy light painted her, a coincidence, he told himself, not the hand of God pointing the way.

"I've had one wife run off on me. I can't have another." He gave the trunk a push, shoving it deeper into the wagon box. "Gertie can't take one more loss."

"Neither can I." The tears standing in her eyes shimmered like pieces of a long-ago broken spirit.

He'd been quick to judge Miss Sawyer based on

her looks, perhaps so quick because he'd feared she would look at him and do the same. Now that he gazed deeper, he saw they were more alike than different. He was sorry for that. He knew what it was to wait for someone to return, refusing to give up hope. He knew what it was like for that hope to die and your soul right along with it.

The chains rattled as he secured the tailgate. He didn't want to face her reaction. Best not to see the disappointment on the woman as she realized in gaining Gertie she would be getting him. "This means you will need to marry me."

"I shall try to endure it." A hint of humor played in her words, her silent message saying she didn't mind too much, and it made the place between his ribs sting unbearably.

He refused to like her. Common sense whispered to him that he was a fool but he helped her step onto the running board, anyway. Gertie would have a ma. A ma he believed would stay.

He hoped he was right as he circled around to his seat and took the reins.

Chapter Three

What am I getting into? She braced herself on the seat as the runners struck another rut. Tate sat as stoic as a mountain, reins in his capable hands, attention on the late-afternoon traffic. She wanted to dislike him except for his words that stuck in her head. *I've had one wife run off on me.*

He'd been abandoned? And Gertie, too? She studied the child's small hand tucked into her own, lost in the too-large glove. Felicity sighed. That explained why he'd been unsure about her. He'd been trying to protect his child. Her child, now. She would not fault him for that. She'd never seen anyone with so much pain in him.

Festive candles flickered in shop windows, decorated for Christmas. This day that should have been filled with promise; she only felt a strange ache settling deep into her chest, refusing to budge. Perhaps her optimism had been a tad high for a mail-order bride. She thought of Eleanor McBride, the young woman she'd befriended on the train. When they'd discovered they were both journeying to marry men they'd never met, they had struck up an instant bond. Eleanor had disembarked at Dry Creek while she'd gone on to Angel Falls, and during that last leg of her journey she had time to imagine an awful lot. But she hadn't been prepared for the real Tate Winters. Had Eleanor's experience been similar? Eleanor's groom had not met her at the train.

Her teeth clacked together as the runners hit an extremely bumpy rut. *He needs to get to know me better,* she decided. Maybe once he saw who she was and how much this family meant to her, things would be different. Stubborn hope struggled for life as she dared to study him out of the corners of her eyes. Severe, he looked like a sculpture carved out of pure marble. How would a smile change his face? She pictured his unforgiving lines softening with humor and his midnight-blue eyes dancing with laughter.

Her stomach fluttered and not from nerves. She held on to the edge of the seat as the horse drew them over a small berm and into a side street, where twilight turned shadows into darkness. Tate became a silhouette, an impressive outline of masculinity and might, and the flutter moved upward toward her heart. He would be quite handsome, she guessed, if hopelessness didn't rest so heavily on his iron shoulders.

"That's the feed store where Pa works." Gertie pointed out as the runners jounced onto the next street. The lighted windows of storefronts reflected warmly on the long stretch of ice. "It's Uncle Devin's store. It used to be Grandpop's store, but he died."

Felicity caught a glimpse of a barrel behind the shop's window before Patches drew them onto a residential street. She glanced around. Not exactly a prosperous place. One tiny shanty slumped in the darkness. Another one peered at them from behind a grove of scrawny trees.

"And that's where we live. Right there. Do you see it?"

"It's too dark." She leaned forward, straining through the thickening duskiness. Emotion choked her and stung in her eyes, making it hard to see the dwelling. A lamp burned on the other side of a curtain, casting just enough light to see a crooked porch and lopsided eaves, yellow clapboard and a sturdy front door.

"Now do you see it?"

"I do." No more boardinghouse meals and temporary rooms or a bed that had never been her own. This was her home. Her first real home in seventeen years.

Thank you, Lord. She let the gratitude move through her. Hebrews 11:1 promised hope and a good future, and she'd never felt the words touch her more. Patches nosed down the narrow driveway, drawing them up to the small yellow house, shabby with poverty and neglect.

"It isn't much." Tate's baritone held no note of emotion. He didn't move, a brawny form, radiating a challenge. As if he expected her to find fault or prove him right by deciding to cut her losses and leave now.

Not a chance. He didn't know her well, but he would. When she made up her mind, nothing could sway her. An icy plop fell onto her cheek, accompanied by a hundred taps onto the frozen ground. Snow. Heaven's reassurance. Like grace, snow make things fresh and new.

"This house is just right." She lifted her chin, determined to let Tate see she wasn't going anywhere. "It's the nicest place I've lived in for a long while."

A deep "hmm" resonated from his side of the wagon, as if her answer surprised him. His movements rustled, echoing faintly in the silent stretch of dark as the last dregs of twilight vanished from the sky. Inky blackness descended in full, making Tate a part of the night as his steely hand gripped her elbow, helping her to keep her balance as she sank ankle-deep in snow.

"Careful there." The smoky pitch of his words enveloped her briefly. Unaware of his effect on her he pulled away, leaving her to trudge along a shoveled path toward the porch steps.

"C'mon, Felicity. Follow me." Gertie shivered with anticipation as she charged up the steps. The front door flew open in a wash of lamplight.

"I thought I heard you pull in." A woman about twenty-three or twenty-four, Felicity's same age, came into sight in a carefully patched dress. Her voice had a smiling quality, the sound of a friend. "Goodness, Gertie, don't drag Felicity around like that. Felicity, I'm Ingrid, Tate's sister."

"Sister?" She hadn't known. Gertie hadn't written

of an aunt. She hurried up the steps. "I'm delighted to meet you, Ingrid."

"Call me Ing." Ingrid hauled her through the doorway and into a welcoming hug. "It is wonderful you are finally here. Gertie shared your every letter with me. I've been on pins and needles all day long waiting for you. I think we will be great friends."

"I do, too." Happiness lumped in her throat, making it hard to speak. "I didn't know I was getting a new sister."

"Tate is in real trouble now, since we can conspire against him." Good-humored brown eyes glanced out the open doorway, where a frigid wind gusted and Tate's shadow knelt to lower the trunk onto the tiny porch.

Why did her heart jump at his shadow? Why did she strain to hear the departing crunch of his boots down the pathway? A moment later, horse hooves clinked a slow rhythm, growing faint.

"I'm sure he heard me and didn't like what I said." Laughing, Ingrid closed the door against the wintry night. "Let me hang your coat while you get warm by the fire."

"Shouldn't I fetch my trunk?"

"Tate will bring it in when he's done stabling the horse." Ingrid, petite and slender, apple-cheeked and energetic, helped Felicity out of her wraps. "You must be frozen through. I've heard some of those railroad cars can be quite drafty. Was it exciting riding a train all that way?"

"Very. The most exciting thing I've ever done." She

thought of Eleanor as she surrendered her coat. She glanced around and noted the secondhand sofa with fraying cushions, a scarred wooden chair and a battered table tucked midway between the sitting area and the kitchen. She set her reticule on a rickety end table. "Have you ever ridden the train?"

"Sadly, yes. Many times." Sorrow stole Ingrid's smile as she hung the coats on a wall peg. Even Gertie bowed her head, as if saying anything more would dredge up a sadness neither of them could speak of.

What had happened to this family? Questions burned on her tongue, but she stayed silent, not wanting to sadden them more. The scent of a baking roast rose richly from the range. In the shadows, the kitchen took up the other outside wall of the main room with a pair of tall cupboards and slanting shelves. Wilting muslin curtains hung on the windows, the only adornment in the plain, brown room. This place needed a woman's touch. Good thing she'd spent time sewing, embroidering and crocheting preparing for this day.

"What do you think of Tate?" Ingrid whirled away to light a lamp centered on the round oak table.

"He's—" Words failed her. She thought of his frown. She thought of his cold manner. Then she remembered the love he had for his daughter. "I think he will make a fine husband."

"He will. He is absolutely a good man." Ingrid lifted the lamp's glass chimney and brought a flickering match to the exposed wick. "I'm glad you see that in him."

Gertie sidled close and pulled off the overly large

gloves one by one to watch her aunt light the lamp. The glass chimney clinked back into place like a bell ending the sadness. Light danced, driving the shadows from the room and Felicity was able to see more of her new home. Blue ironware plates sat on shelves, pots and pans rested on lower ones. The windows were large and bound to let in plenty of cheerful sunshine during the day. She could make this place feel cozy in no time.

Bless this house with Your love, Lord. She smiled reassuringly into Gertie's anxious blue eyes. *Help me to make it into a home. That's what Gertie needs.*

She needed it, too.

And Tate? She felt his approach long before the rhythm of his boots reached her. Remembering his desolate shadows, she wondered what she could do for him, this man who had given her this dream of a real home.

"Here are your gloves, Felicity."

"Thank you, Gertie. Do you hear that?"

"It's Pa!" Adoration illuminated her, making her as bright as a star in the heavenly sky. Her shoes tapped a beat to the door, which she flung open. "Pa's got your trunk!"

"So I see." She couldn't explain why her gaze searched the shadows for a glimpse of his face. She longed for the sight of him. The side of her trunk hid him as he lumbered into the reach of lamplight. Without a word he bypassed her and disappeared behind a door in the far wall.

That's it? Not so much as a hello, or where do

you want your trunk? She folded her gloves in half, smoothing them absently. She felt Ingrid's curiosity, and then sympathy as she slipped the gloves next to her reticule. His behavior didn't hurt her, at least that's what she tried to believe. In reality it did, down deep.

A thump echoed through the lifeless rooms as her trunk hit the floor.

"Don't take it personally. Tate doesn't realize how cold he can seem." Ingrid set a steaming teacup on the edge of the table. "Sometimes a heart is broken too many times and there is no way to put it back together again."

Felicity considered those hushed words and her hopes sank. She'd imagined so much with each letter she received from Gertie. A wonderfully loving father, a happy home, a man lonely and in need of a caring wife. She could see now those were Gertie's hopes, not Tate's. It wasn't reality.

His boots struck like hammer blows on the wood floor, his cane tapping a counter rhythm. He shouldered into sight, shrinking the room. He looked immense with his broad shoulders and muscled girth. The power of his disinterest in her struck like a hard gust of wind, shaking her to the bones.

"I gave you my room. I moved all my things across the street, to the room above the store." An icicle would be warmer than his tone and a glacier friendlier. "You will live here with Gertie until we're...married... and then I'll move into the lean-to."

"Won't that get rather cold?"

"Probably." A muscle jumped along his jaw line,

a sign of strain. She hadn't considered how hard this must be for a man to take on a wife he clearly didn't want.

She felt numb, suffocating in disappointment. How many times had she imagined this moment? Walking into her new home to see the happy future she and Gertie and Tate would share? She'd pictured every outcome but this one, full of awkwardness and the feeling of being unwanted. She had made a terrible mistake.

She'd also made the right one. Gertie twisted her hands, a worried little girl in a wash-worn calico dress.

Is this why You brought me here, Father? She didn't need God's answer to know it was true. Tate's heart might be irrevocably broken, but Gertie's spirit was beautiful, fragile and immeasurably precious.

"Tate." Ingrid's scolding tone held disappointment, too. "I can't believe you. She's going to change her mind about marrying you."

"I told her that to reassure her." The muscle twisted in his jaw, harder this time. "She has a place, respectful to her reputation as I promised."

"You could have said it more gently." Ingrid shook her head, brown curls scattering. "You're going to scare her into leaving."

"But you said she would stay." Gertie took her father's hand, small and frail standing next to the large, powerful man.

"I'm right here, Gertie." Felicity resisted the urge to rush to the child and wrap her in her arms. Commitment turned her to steel. "I don't want you worrying, okay?"

"Okay." The child gulped, holding on to her father with white-knuckled need. Was she afraid he would leave her, too? Hadn't she said something about being separated from Tate? Felicity swiped a lock of hair out of her burning eyes. Just what had happened to this family?

"Ingrid, thank you." She turned to her sister-to-be and squeezed her hand. "You've made me feel at home."

"I did nothing but introduce myself and make you some tea. What I want is for you to put up your feet, rest up from your long journey and let me whip up the rest of supper—"

"That is my job." She could read Ingrid's worry, saw it crinkle across her smooth brow, and understood. Tate's sister wanted to smooth the way, fearing any woman in her right mind would flee. What would life be like being married to a man who said he had no gentleness or heart left in him?

"I appreciate all you've done, Ingrid, but I have been looking forward to making supper for my new family." She hated to trouble the woman further. "Maybe we could talk tomorrow. I could fix you lunch."

"I would love it." Ingrid's smile was a mix of delight and wariness when she studied the man in the shadows. With a sigh she reached for her coat. "You behave, Tate. I'll see you at noon, Felicity. I'm *so* glad you came."

"Me, too. Good night." Purpose held her up. Tate's boots struck once, twice and a third step took him to the potbellied stove in the sitting area. The door rattled and squeaked open. As Gertie hugged her aunt and saw her to the door, Tate shoveled coal from the hod. His wide back to her, he worked quietly and efficiently.

"Felicity?" Gertie stood before her, anxiety puckering her adorable face. Golden curls framed her fathomless eyes full of a sadness no child should know.

She understood the silent question and tore her gaze from the solemn man adjusting the stove's draft. "Everything is fine. I see Ingrid was getting ready to peel potatoes. Would you like to keep me company in the kitchen?"

"I'll show you where the cutting board is." Eager to please, the girl bobbed away, braids bouncing.

Across the length of the room, she felt Tate's curiosity. When she raised her gaze to his, he turned away, staring hard at the floor. His thick, dark hair fell beyond his collar, straggling and too long. The flannel collar was fraying, too. Everywhere she looked needed needle and thread—the sofa cushions, Gertie's sleeve, even the dish towel where the washed potatoes sat on the edge of the table.

"Here." Gertie bent to yank something off the bottom shelf, accidentally bumping a pan. It tumbled onto the floor with an ear-ringing clatter. Startled, the girl jumped as if struck. "I'm sorry. I didn't mean to."

"It's all right." She knelt to retrieve the pan. "No harm done. We'll just give it a good swipe with a dish cloth and it will be as good as new. Is that the cutting board?"

Obviously it was, but Gertie clutched the slab of wood tighter with both arms, eyes silent with distress. In her years at the orphanage, she'd witnessed many sadnesses. Remembering that Gertie had been parted from her father and not knowing what had happened in the time between, she gently laid her hand against the child's soft, apple cheek. Inalterable love whispered in her heart for this little girl in need. Not only in need of love but of healing.

"Do you want to put the pieces in the pot for me? I always used to help my ma that way."

Gertie swallowed hard, visibly struggling, and nodded. Just once.

"Then let's pick out the right pot. Does this look like a good size to you, or do you want more potatoes? Maybe this one?"

"That's the one." Gertie hugged the cutting board against her chest with one arm and held out her free hand, as if determined to help by carrying both.

Felicity handed over the potato pot to her child, her own little girl. How many times over the years had she wished for such a blessing? Overwhelmed, she rose on shaky knees, surprised when Tate's hand caught her elbow to help her up. She hadn't heard his approach but he towered over her, blocking the pool of light. Big and intimidating, but it was kindness she glimpsed.

He might deny it, but she saw it chase the dark hues from his eyes and the rocky harshness from the planes of his chiseled face.

"Thank you." His gaze collided with hers. Maybe it was the trick of the flickering light behind him or the depth of the shadows he stood in, but his coldness melted. Apology shone in his eyes and the authenticity of it rolled through her, hooking deep into her heart. His cane tapped a beat as he stepped away. The lamplight washed over her, the moment passed but the hook remained.

"I'll fetch more coal for you." Once again cold and unreachable, the man scooped up the hod by the range and limped away.

"Thanks." She helped Gertie slide the pot onto the table. As the cutting board thunked to a rest, she watched the bob of Tate's invincible shoulders rise and fall with his uneven gait until the shadows stole him from her sight. The ring of his boots on the floor continued, his cane in counterpoint.

Maybe he wasn't as unreachable as she'd thought. A small hope flared to life within her. It was a small light in a vast dark but it was enough to see. Coming here was no mistake.

Chapter Four

He glimpsed her through a crack between the curtains, embraced by lamplight, sipping from a cup as she stood in front of the stove, her back to him. Her golden hair was wrapped around her head like a coronet in one long braid. Her yellow dress accentuated her woman's form, delicate shoulders, slim waist, flaring skirt that draped gracefully to the floor. The light seemed to search her out; like finding like. Gertie was right. The woman did look like a fairy-tale princess out of a book.

What had he gotten himself into? His stomach clenched with foreboding as he forced his bad leg forward and stabbed his cane into the snow. Airy flakes sailed around him, the first harbingers of a coming storm. He figured more snow to shovel and wrestle through was no hardship compared to dealing with the woman in his kitchen, stirring something in a pan. Gertie loved her. That was what mattered. The only thing that sustained him as he forced his feet toward the house. It was going to be torture to get used to having that woman in his house.

"Pa!" The door flung open the instant he stomped snow from his boots. A grinning Gertie filled the threshold, her rosebud smile a welcome sight. "Guess what? Felicity let me help make the biscuits."

"That's good." He cupped the side of her cherub cheek, his dear girl. He saw the tiny newborn cradled in his arms, the gentle toddler wobbling as she took her first steps, the withered child sobbing when the marshal had taken him away. He cleared unwanted emotion from his throat. "I'm sure I'm going to like those biscuits."

His words must have carried to the woman because she turned from the stove to greet him with a soft look. Gentle. Something he hadn't seen outside of his family in a long while and his windpipe closed up. He stared back at her, probably looking like a lumbering fool, unable to say a word.

"I'm just finishing up the gravy, otherwise supper is ready." She offered him a sunny smile before turning to the stove. "I used to help out in the dining room where I lived, for a discount of my room and board. I love to cook."

"These are the biscuits, Pa." Gertie pranced up to the table and pointed to a bowl, neatly wrapped in a dish towel to hold the heat inside. "They taste real good. I ate some of the crumbled-off pieces."

"I can't wait to have one." His voice came out strained and coarse, the best he could manage. He shrugged out of his coat, focusing too hard on hanging up the garment just so he didn't have to look at the woman. He was going to have to start thinking of her with a name.

"It was so thoughtful of your sister to start supper." Her brisk steps went from stove to table, tap, tap, tapping like a dance. "I see she cleaned, too. You have a brother also?"

He nodded. Took a reluctant step toward the table. "Devin."

"He owns the feed store where you work. I have it straight now." She set two plates on the table and whirled to fetch more.

His stomach growled harder, the food did look tasty. Thick peppery gravy and a fluffy white mountain of mashed potatoes with butter melting down the peak. Gertie's eyes shone as she pulled out her chair.

For Gertie, he found the strength to sit down at the table. A cup of tea steamed beside his plate, waiting to warm him. He peered through his lashes as the woman—as Felicity— added a platter and a bowl to the table.

"Can I get you anything else? I hope I didn't forget something." Her warm pleasantness felt out of place in this sad house.

"It's just right, Felicity," Gertie breathed, still in awe of the woman. "It's perfect."

Do it for Gertie, he told himself again, finding the strength he'd lacked before to offer the woman— Felicity—a half smile. "This looks very good."

"Looks can be deceiving," she quipped, settling into the chair across the small table from him. "I can only hope you think it tastes just as good. Who usually leads the prayer?"

"I do." Gertie's hand crept into his, holding on tight. Her head bowed, her eyes squeezed shut in earnest belief, she began the blessing. "Dear Father."

Warm fingers curled around his other hand. The shock of the woman's touch hammered through him. Gertie's blessing became garbled, words he could not make sense of as Felicity bowed her head. Lamplight caressed her porcelain perfection, accentuating her beauty. Her hand tucked in his felt dainty, as fine-boned as a bird's.

"Thank You so much for my new ma," Gertie prayed on. "Now everything will be all right, I just know it. Amen."

"Amen," he muttered. He tried to ignore the pinch of regret when he released hold of the woman. His hand felt empty. Out of the corner of his eye he watched her reach for a platter and angled it in his direction as an offering.

Her gaze did something to him. It pulled at him down deep, and so he avoided it. He did take the roast beef. He speared several slices with his fork, realizing too late she'd given him first choice. He wanted to read something into her gesture; Lolly always had a motive behind every action, but he could not get up the steam to suspect Felicity of the same.

"Don't forget the biscuits, Pa." Gertie slid the bowl in his direction.

"I won't." He added a slice to her plate. "Those biscuits are all I can think about."

"Put lots of butter on 'em."

"That was my plan." He chose a couple biscuits from the bowl and cracked them open with his knife. Buttermilk goodness, crumbly and fragrant made his mouth water. At least he would be eating well. Another reason to be grateful for his wife-to-be. "You ladies did a real fine job."

"I stirred up the batter." Gertie dug into the mashed potatoes and spooned a mound onto her plate. "I put them into the oven, too."

"She was a fantastic helper." Felicity reached for the gravy. "I think we make a great team."

"Me, too." With an emphatic nod, the girl thunked the potato bowl onto the table.

"What do you both like for breakfast? I need to know for when the morning rolls around. Maybe there are some things I should avoid making. Like rhubarb pancakes."

"Ick." Gertie curled her upper lip, eyes dancing. "There's no such thing as rhubarb pancakes."

"Tell that to the cook at the orphanage. A patron donated a sizable portion of rhubarb from her gardens and not one bit of it went to waste. We had mashed rhubarb, chopped rhubarb, minced rhubarb. We had rhubarb in bread, in oatmeal, in meat loaf and stew. The pancakes were the best of the bunch, almost edible."

"No rhubarb pancakes." Gertie laughed. The melody of it rose above the rumble of the fire in the stove and chased the chill from the room. The most beautiful sound.

"Okay, then I'll cross that off the list. Anything else? How about charred eggs? Burned bacon?"

"No, don't make that, either." The child's cheeks shone pink with delight. "I don't like things burned."

"Good to know. I'll try not to scorch anything." She swirled her fork in the potatoes on her plate. "Does that mean you like things undercooked? Like wilty bacon? Runny eggs?"

"Nope." Gertie nibbled on the edge of a biscuit. "Just do it all the regular way."

"I'll do my best." She considered the stoic man across the table, head bent, cutting the beef and stabbing it with his fork. He had to be listening. "Any special requests, Tate?"

"Me?" His head jerked up, dark locks tumbling over his high forehead, giving him a rakish look.

A handsome look. For a brief moment she saw him differently. Confident, gentle and whole. What an impressive man he must have been. He still must be, she decided.

"Whatever you cook is fine." His fork stopped midair. "I appreciate not having to make it myself."

"So you do the cooking." The picture was coming clear. Tate standing at the stove, trying to do both the work of a mother and a father. "I thought maybe Ingrid did."

"No. My sister has her own life. I do my best not to impose on her." The words lashed and he winced. Obviously he hadn't meant to be harsh. "Sorry. It's an argument in my family. They did so much for Gertie while I was…away."

He choked on that last word, and Felicity wondered why. Sorrow filled the air. She wanted to know what had happened but now wasn't the time. She would leave that sadness for another day. "I hope you don't mind if she and I are friendly. I've been without my sisters for so long I ache for that connection again. When I met her, I thought perhaps we could be close, like real sisters should be."

"I'm sure she will like that." One corner of his mouth curled upward. Bleakness faded from his eyes' midnight-blue depths. "Ingrid has been nearly as excited by your arrival as Gertie is. My sister will probably want to drag you with her to her social events. I don't have a problem with that. You should make friends here."

"Oh. Friends." She hadn't thought that far. Suddenly a whole new world opened up to her. The lonely existence she'd left behind faded. She was no longer alone. Did Tate realize what he had done for her?

"It must be hard leaving everything behind." He peered at her from behind his dark lashes. "And everyone."

"There was no one left, not toward the end. The friends I'd made at work left town when they lost their jobs. The relationships I'd made at the orphanage didn't last. Most of the girls I grew up with were eager to put the past behind them and went somewhere else to start fresh." She shrugged. Staying had been her choice, so it wasn't a sad thing. "I wasn't able to let go."

"What work did you do?"

"I'm a seamstress." She liked that he wanted to know about her. Surely that was a good sign? He was reaching out to her and it made the small hope within her grow. "When I was a girl, I was hired out one summer to sew in a workshop in Cedar Rapids. It was an unpleasant circumstance, but I worked hard at learning the craft. When I was sent back to the or-phanage in September, I had the skills I needed to find a job when I was old enough."

"How old were you?"

"Eleven. And that's just what I did. I worked hard to improve my sewing and when I was on my own, I worked in a dress shop making beautiful things."

"That explains your clothes. That's no calico work dress."

"I wanted to make a good impression, so you wouldn't take one look at me and wish me back on that train." Her smile wobbled, though she tried to hide it. Guilt hit him because that was just what he'd wanted.

Not anymore. He took another bite of a delicious biscuit and followed it up with a flavorful mouthful of potato and gravy. Hard to swallow past the lump in his throat but he managed it. Felicity Sawyer was not what she seemed, not at all. His daughter had done a fine job picking out a ma. He wasn't much of a pro-vider, probably wouldn't be much of a husband, but he vowed to do his best.

Gertie wasn't the only one who deserved it.

"Do you know what time it is?" Felicity studied Gertie over the rim of her teacup. The meal was nearly done, Tate polished off the last biscuit on his plate and she recognized the girl's fidgety excitement on her seat.

"Is it present time?" She lost the battle and bobbed off her chair. The question furrowed her dear brow and pleaded like a wish in her eyes. Such an adorable child. Felicity felt as if she'd always loved her.

"I don't know about you, but I can't wait a moment longer. Let's go fetch your gifts." She set down her cup with a clink, rising to her feet. Aware of Tate's steady gaze, she dropped the napkin onto the table and followed Gertie's dancing steps from the lighted room.

The farthest door opened into a small bedroom. Inky hints of a headboard and a window were all she could see before her right shoe bumped against her trunk. Surely there had to be a lamp here somewhere. She heard Tate's boots approach, illumination spilled into the room bobbing closer as he did and her surroundings came to life. A bed against one wall, a shabby chest of drawers against another and a pair of muslin curtains, that was all. Not even an extra lamp.

"I put your gift right on top." Felicity knelt beside her trunk, where Gertie already waited, squirming with anticipation, and worked the latch on the lid. "I started making it as soon as I read your first letter. That's how much I liked you."

Anticipation beat, making her hand tremble and her pulse thumped, heavy and syrupy in her veins as she opened the lid. Tate leaned in with the lamp and set it on the chest of drawers behind her. His nearness shrank the room and made skittles on her skin, like a summer breeze blowing.

"Felicity, is that really for me?" The girl gasped, unbelieving.

She opened her mouth but no answer came. She had lost every word she knew. Was it because of the solemn man towering over her? He was enormous from this vantage, sculpted muscle and powerful masculinity, a mountain of a man made of granite. His face was a mask of rock but his gaze softened when he looked into the trunk. His eyes turned glassy, as if overcome with emotion.

"Is she really mine?" Gertie repeated, as if certain she was dreaming. As if the gift could not be real.

"She's yours. I didn't name her. I thought you could do that. Go ahead and hold her."

"Oh. She's beautiful." Golden ringlets bounced as the girl bent down to gather the cloth doll into her arms like a mother holding a new baby. She simply stared into the doll's face, taking in the embroidered rosebud mouth and blue button eyes.

"I wanted her to look like you." She couldn't resist brushing back a wayward ringlet, as soft as the finest silk. Love for this precious girl deepened. "I didn't know if you already had a doll."

Gertie shook her head, curls bobbing, and the silence became sorrow. The same emotion etched into Tate's stony features. When his gaze captured hers, his stoniness eased. He nodded once, his appreciation clear.

She wasn't aware of removing another gift from the

trunk or rising to face the man. The force in his eyes held her captive, impossible to look away. The hook in her heart deepened, its grip on her secure. Why did it feel as if she were falling? She stood perfectly straight, her balance was just fine. Yet the room tilted until the only steady thing was Tate's midnight gaze holding her in place.

"This is for you." Her hands felt disconnected from the rest of her as she held out the woolen bundle. When his eyes broke from hers to study the gift she offered him, she felt oddly bereft, alone and full of loss. As if without the binding connection of his gaze, she was no longer the same, no longer whole. The room stopped whirling. The ground steadied beneath her feet. Uncertainty wound through her as Tate's rocky mask returned. So remote, she could not read his reaction.

Did he not like the scarf? She'd knitted it during the empty hours after supper and before bed, needles clacking, wondering about the man she was making it for. "I guessed at the color. I didn't know what you liked."

"It will do." His baritone grated, rough and hard as if he were angry but that wasn't the emotion creasing his face. The show of feeling was brief before it vanished. "I appreciate it."

"I hoped the blue would match your eyes." She felt inadequate standing before him and she didn't know why. Perhaps she'd secretly wished the gift of a scarf would break the ice between them, take them from being strangers to something more friendly.

"I have nothing to give to you." Apology cracked the crevice of stone. Another clue to the mystery of the man.

"Nothing?" Couldn't he see what he'd done? "You bought me a train ticket. You brought me here. I will have a whole new life and a family because of you."

"You aren't disappointed?" He folded the scarf, concentrating on the task, ill at ease. "This can't be what you expected."

"No." Her loving gaze fell on Gertie, still kneeling on the floor. "It's a great deal more than I'd hoped."

"You are, too." The words made him feel way too vulnerable and he knew he was heading for trouble. There could be no tie between him and the woman. Just a convenient arrangement for the child's sake. But he wanted Felicity to know she was wanted here. For what she'd already done for Gertie, she'd earned his devotion. Likely as not, her opinion of him would change over time when she heard the rumors about him and learned they were largely true.

But for now he let her smile wash through him, as rare as a Christmas star. He knew God looking down from His heaven had not forgotten Gertie. Tate was grateful. The child tipped her face up to beam at her new mother.

"Thank you so, so much." Eyes brimming, the girl hugged the doll tight. "I will love her *forever.*"

He took his leave, swallowed hard against the painful lump lodged in his throat and headed for the chair by the fire. He had work waiting, something to keep his mind busy and his thoughts on the practical. He was no dreamer. Life had taught him the hard way dreams were for the foolish. Once he'd been a fool dreaming of happiness, seeing the best in folks, even where it could not possibly exist. He paid a high price for that lesson he must never forget.

Not even a beautiful woman and her gift of a rag doll with yarn hair and a pink calico dress could make him believe. How could she have known about the doll? He stared at the scarf clutched in one hand, the yarn soft and warm. Voices lifted and fell cheerfully as the females discussed one dress after another while unpacking that heavy trunk. He didn't have to look to know Gertie still clutched her doll in both arms good and tight, as if it were the grandest treasure in all the world.

He wrapped the length of wool around his neck. Soft, it smelled faintly of roses, the way Felicity did. His chest tangled into a thousand knots as he shrugged into his coat and closed his ears to the sound of the woman's gentle laughter. But it was too late. The trill of happiness echoed inside him, in the places so empty not even his soul could live there.

He opened the door and took refuge in the dark, in the cold that froze the feeling from his face and fingers, and in the night that cloaked him. Like a ghost, he trudged across the road, surrounded by darkly gleaming snow and a faint echo of her laughter that clung inside him and refused to let go.

Chapter Five

Would Tate come back? Felicity held the plate up to catch the lamplight, gave it a final swipe with the soapy cloth and, satisfied, swirled it around in the rinse basin. It clinked lightly to a rest on top of the others. Alone in the main room, she glanced toward the door. He wasn't a talkative fellow, so perhaps he'd gone across the street for the night and she would need to bank the fires. Surely he would be returning for breakfast in the morning?

She turned to scoop the potato pot into the wash basin. Water splashed and sloshed as she scrubbed at the mealy residue left along the sides of the pan. Gertie slept with Merry, her doll, tucked in both arms. How sweet it had been to listen to the child's prayers, to straighten her blankets and kiss her forehead. The coziness lingered even in the silence and the echo of her every step on the floorboards. This day had gone much better than expected in some ways. She thought of Eleanor and wondered if her husband-to-be had ever shown up to meet her. She prayed Eleanor had fared at least as well.

The front door ripped open, startling her. The pot slipped from her fingers and splatted into the water. Soap bubbles burst into flight, iridescent in the lamplight.

"Thought I'd come help out now that my work is done. I still had some deliveries to make." He closed the door with one shoulder, moving stiffly. Snow dusted his wide shoulders. Cold clung to him and he brought the chill inside as he shrugged off his coat. "That scarf came in handy."

"I'm glad." At least she had made one small difference for him. She gave the pan another good swipe. "It's gotten a lot colder out there. Is the room above the store warm?"

"Warm enough." He lumbered into the light, the dark shadows accentuating the creases on his face time and hardship had worn into him. "It was a thoughtful thing you did for Gertie in making her that doll."

"My pleasure." A strange shivery feeling swept through her as he sidled closer. Her husband-to-be. He leaned his cane against the table and stole a folded dish towel from the nearby stack. She wanted to like this man. No—she wanted to love him. Caring flickered hopefully in her heart as she studied his granite profile. Such a hard man with such a gentle love for his daughter.

"I had so much fun making each stitch just right and trying to figure out what Gertie would like." She let him take the pan from her and dunk it into the rinse water. "My ma made a doll for the three of us, me and my sisters."

"What happened to them? Why aren't you with them?" Water dripped from the pan as he wrapped it in a towel and began to dry.

"My youngest sister was adopted right away. It tore me apart to watch her go." She squeezed her eyes shut briefly against the crushing pain, grief still strong after seventeen years. "A kindly looking couple took her, so I have hopes that she was treasured. Faith and I were together until I was eleven."

"When you were hired out?"

"Yes. When I came back she was gone. Hired out and never returned. We didn't know what became of her." She gave the pot lid a good scour. "As far as I could find out, another family eventually took her for home care. The same thing happened to me later that year. I wound up working on a pig farm to earn my keep."

"You didn't learn all you could about pigs to become a farmer later?"

Was that the tiniest glimmer of humor warming the chill from his rumbling words? Did Tate Winters have a sense of humor buried in there somewhere? Pleased, she slid the lid into the rinse water and reached for the final pan. "Surprisingly, no. That was one smelly opportunity I let pass me by."

"I don't blame you. I delivered feed to the Rutger place tonight." He deftly dried the pot until it shone. "Pig farm."

She chuckled but she laughed alone. Tate no longer seemed as formidable. "I didn't expect help with the dishes."

"I don't mind. We need to talk."

"Yes, we do." What a relief. She plunged both hands into the hot water to scrub the roasting pan. *Do you think you can love me?* That's what she wanted to ask. "There is so much we need to figure out together. The wedding for one."

"I've spoken to the town reverend. He has time before the Christmas Eve service."

"Gertie will be pleased." She worked the dish-cloth into the pan's greasy corners. "In her letters she wanted us to get married by Christmas."

"Yes, and as you can see there is not a lot of money to spare." The muscle jumped in his jaw again. He held himself so rigid and tense she had to wonder what he expected her to say. To berate him? To think less of him because he was so poor? How could she think less of a man who loved his daughter so much?

"I have a dress to wear. My Sunday best should do." She gave the pan a measuring look but he took it from her before she could determine if it met her cleanliness standards. His hands were capable and callused and a long thin scar disappeared into the cuff of his sleeve. His flannel shirt wanted mending, too, and she hung her head. How much hardship had the rail ticket caused him? "There should be no need for further expenses."

"Gertie should have a new dress." He swallowed

hard, his impressive shoulders tense. "If you're a seamstress, could I ask you to sew her one?"

"I saved up several lengths of fabric, hoping I might be able to sew for her, for my daughter." He probably had no idea what those words meant to her. They warmed the lonely places in her soul, they made the losses of her parents, and then her sisters, fade. "How about you? I'm fairly skilled at men's garments."

"I don't pretend to be something I'm not. I have no need of fancy new duds or the money to afford them." The muscle in his jaw jumped, strung tighter, and drew up cords of tendons in his neck. She could feel his raw pain like a wind gust to the lamp, dampening the light.

"Maybe sometime later, when things are better." She wrung the extra water from her cloth and wiped the table. "I had hoped to keep my sewing skills polished. After I'm done sewing for Gertie, I could ask around in town. Maybe find some piece work at one of the local dress shops. I don't want my needle to go rusty."

"That's good of you but not necessary. You take care of Gertie. That's our bargain." He could hardly breathe as he rinsed the roasting pan, the sloshing sound hiding the wheeze in his chest. Shame wrapped around him. She was as beautiful on the inside as she was in the lamplight. He did not deserve her. She did not deserve what folks would be saying about the woman who married him.

He set the pan down too hard. The clatter punctuated the harsh cast to his words, made harder by the fading light. The lamp needed more kerosene. "You don't need to pay your way, Felicity."

"That's the first time you've said my name."

Hope. He hadn't been without it so long that he'd forgotten the sound of it. He hung his head, unable to look at her. A terrible feeling settled in his gut. He put the pan on the shelf, grateful for the break away from her. The lamplight writhed, struggling for life, casting eerie orange flickers along the wall. "I suppose I can't call you Miss Sawyer for much longer."

"No, as I will soon be Mrs. Winters. Huh. That's the first time I've said that." She circled the table in the lengthening shadows, swiping up every last crumb, a swirl of color and sweetness. "I like it. It makes me feel as if I belong here."

She filled the house with a force that did not fade as the flame gave one last thrash and sputtered out. The last thing he saw clearly was the plea in her lovely eyes.

A plea. His guts twisted tight as he spun on his heel, plodding by memory to the lean-to entrance. He fumbled in the dark and not because he couldn't find his way. Her plea stayed with him like a noose about his neck. Something he couldn't outrun. Something that tightened around his throat cruelly.

The woman hadn't come here expecting some romantic fairy tale, had she? He snatched the kerosene can off the shelf, his grip so tight on his cane his skin burned. That wasn't what he'd signed up for. That wasn't something he could do. He knew where love led. He was still picking up the shattered pieces of that illusion. Bitterness soured his mouth, tore through him like winter lightning and he stumbled back into the kitchen where the faint scent of roses, of her, softened the darkness.

"Gertie said you work tomorrow. Should I expect you home for lunch? What would you like for supper?"

Her kindness became cruel, but she couldn't know that. She meant well. Her helpfulness and concern glanced off the glacier his soul had become. He wished he had some kindness to offer her in return. He removed the glass chimney with a clink as it landed on the table top and twisted open the can. He ignored the pungent smell as he tipped the can, listening to hear when the reservoir sounded full. What he heard was Felicity. The pattern of her step, the drops of water as she doused and wrung out the cloth, the steady nearly nonexistent rhythm of her breathing. Her plea remained, tighter around his neck.

He could not be what she wanted. He was sorry for it. Once he was a man of deep feeling. Prison had torn the feeling right out of him, leaving only the shell. He hated the emptiness inside as he watched her pour the soapy water into the rinse basin. She bent to the task, making a lovely picture. Gleaming, light blond hair, ivory skin, the graceful angle of her slender arm, the way her perfect top teeth worked into her bottom lip as she shook out the last few stubborn drops.

"I'm fortunate to have found you." He had to be honest. It was the best thing he could do for her. He winced, hating to do it, wishing he had some gentleness inside to use to soften the blow. He took the heavy, water-filled basin, lifting it from the table so she wouldn't have to. He swallowed hard, searching for the right words. "Not every woman is sensible enough to agree to marriage the way we have. A business arrangement. A living arrangement. A mutual agreement to make a child's life better."

He hardened himself for her reaction. As his words sank in, the brightness shining within her dimmed a notch. Hope faded, leaving a hollow smile and a tiny gasp of pain she could not hide.

"Nothing more." He searched her, emphasizing those words, waiting for understanding to play across the perfect blue hue of her eyes. "It was what we agreed to before you came."

It was better to be honest, rather than letting her hopes get too high. She had to see the man he was, the failure he'd become. She had to see he had nothing inside of him to give. That did not mean he would not work hard to provide the best life he could for her, for Gertie.

"I'd best get to bed. Work starts early in the morning." The words felt torn from him.

"What time would you like breakfast?" Her strained voice struggled to disguise her disappointment.

He'd hurt her. He hated it but what else could he do? Let her hopes rise higher, only to fall further? He resisted the urge to reach out and brush a wayward curl from her cheek. Silly urge, wanting to bridge the distance between them. A distance that had to remain. That always had to be. He turned on his heel. "I start work at six."

"Five-thirty, then?" She cleared her throat but layers of heartache remained as unmistakable as the shadows. Not even the growing strength of the lamp could chase it away. "I'll have food on the table."

"Thank you." He hesitated at the door, mountain-strong but no longer as remote. "It's been a long time since there's been a woman around, aside from Ingrid. I'll do my best to be gentle."

"We both have some adjusting to do. I'm not used to being around a man." Her boardinghouse had been for women only. How did she explain suitors tended to bypass her just like those prospective parents in the orphanage yard, always choosing another? She hung up the wet dishcloth, ignoring the stinging behind her eyes. "Is there anything more I can do for you to-night?"

"No." Surprise skimmed his face, then furrows of thought dug in. "Good night."

The shadows claimed him as he opened the door. Cold curled in as if to snatch the man out into the dark. With a final thump the door closed, leaving her alone. The wind and snowfall masked the sound of his gait. The stove lid rattled as another gust broadsided the little house, making her pulse skip.

This wasn't what she'd imagined. She gripped the lamp's handle carefully and took it with her from table to couch. The rustle of her petticoats, the swish of her skirt, the pad of her shoes echoed around her. No, this was not what she'd expected when she'd made the decision to accept Tate's briefly written proposal. Not at all what she'd risked dreaming of riding the train westward across the territory.

How could she have been so wrong? Agony twisted through her. With a sigh, she set the lamp next to the sofa and sat. She buried her face in her hands. She'd risked everything coming here hoping for love, a love that could not possibly be found.

A business arrangement. A living arrangement. Nothing more. Tate's words came back to her now, replaying over and over again in her mind. The man she'd imagined didn't exist. He didn't want to care about her. He never would. Her precious hopes fell like glass and shattered all around her into tiny shards and bits of dust that glimmered mockingly in the light.

Her fault for wishing love might grow, anyway. Her heart swelled with pain as she straightened and took a steadying breath. She tugged her yarn basket closer, glad she'd thought to unpack it earlier, and took up her needles and a skein of red Christmas yarn. Gertie needed mittens.

Gertie's love kept her going as she made a slip knot. She cast on stitch after stitch and while she worked the click of steel needles echoed in the vast stillness of the tiny house. The loneliness wrapping around her had never been so huge.

"What's she like?" The question rose out of the dark like a gunshot, startling him.

Tate's cane flew out of his hand, hit the floor and reverberated like cannon fire through the feed store's back room. A match flared to life. "Devin, what are you doing sitting here in the dark?"

"A gust of wind blew out the light."

A glass chimney rattled as his older brother touched flame to wick. Illumination crept across the small worktable, crossed an opened ledger and fell onto the floor at Tate's feet. He bent stiffly to fetch his cane. His injuries ached sorely from the cold and rising storm. "You don't fool me. You're hanging around pretending to do your books late so you can hear all about the woman."

"What if I am?" Devin leaned back in the captain's chair, grinning wide. "I heard all about her from Ingrid. Pretty, blonde, nice. Brother, the good Lord is watching over you because what were the chances you would get someone like that?"

"The good Lord was watching over *Gertie*," he corrected, seizing the cane's grip. The distaste of what'd he been forced to say to Felicity rankled in his chest.

"C'mon, you've got to be relieved." Devin had that tell-me-more look on his face. Clearly he was tickled pink by the turn of events.

"Whether she's pretty or ugly makes no difference to me." He unbuttoned his coat, brushing off snow.

"That can't be true. It would matter to me."

"Yeah? Well, I'm not you. Fortunately." He didn't joke much these days but he still had a drop of humor left somewhere inside. He almost grinned. "Say, tell me again why you aren't married yet?"

"No sensible woman would have me." It was their standard joke and Devin shrugged, leaned farther back in his chair and propped his feet on the edge of the desk. "Ing sure liked her."

"Ing likes everyone." He saw again the hurt and disappointment and Felicity's struggle to hide it. The intangible noose remained around his neck, pulling tighter. He'd done his best tonight. He couldn't resurrect the man he used to be. That man was gone, beaten near to death years ago. He hung his coat on a peg. "She made Gertrude a doll."

"Whew." Impressed, Devin sat up straight. "Figure that's a sign from heaven?"

"I figure it's a sign she is the right woman. She loves Gertie. It's quite a doll. She must have spent a lot of time sewing on it." He swallowed hard, wondering what Felicity was doing right now. Was she still looking shell-shocked? Or had she recovered? He hated to think of her alone and hurting. In time, she would be grateful to him but for now... He blew out a hurting sigh. "Best get upstairs. Morning rolls around fast."

"That it does." Devin searched for a pencil amid the paperwork. "Good night, little brother."

"'Night." He made his way up the stairs through the dark and into the room tucked beneath the peak of the roof. Warmth remained from the heat of the stovepipe spearing through and he lit a battered lantern.

Alone in the half light he sat on the edge of the narrow bed, the straw tick crinkling beneath his weight. He kicked off his left boot. Where did his mind go? To the woman and the gift she'd given Gertie. There hadn't been money enough to replace the one taken from her. Until he'd lowered his pride and accepted help from his brother, he had been desperate. No one wanted to hire a convicted felon, and those who did weren't pleasant to work for and did not pay well.

Just how long would it be before Felicity learned the truth from some town gossip? He raked his hands through his hair and snow sifted downward onto the blankets. He should tell her first, he decided. Perhaps he should have simply blurted it out tonight.

He wanted to say that bringing her here had been a bad decision, but it wasn't. No matter what, he knew that for sure. He just needed to keep his distance and to let the girl and woman bond. Gertie needed her. And that woman full of sweetness and a heart ready to love needed Gertie as much.

At least he prayed it was true. He bowed his head, a man who knew for a fact God had turned His back on him, and prayed.

Chapter Six

The cold bedroom shivered around her as she pinned up her braid. An Iowa girl, she was used to frigid mornings but this one was made worse by nerves. They popped in her stomach as she buttoned up. Facing Tate wasn't going to be easy but after a good night's sleep and more than a little prayer, she felt stronger. One more hairpin and her braid was secure. She gave one last look in the mirror and lifted her chin, ready to face the day. Except for the hurt in her eyes, she looked the same. No other outward sign she was hurting.

Good. The last thing she wanted Tate to know how hurt she was. A girl had her pride. Her primping done, she took the lamp from the chest and opened her door the same moment the front door burst wide in a blaze of ice and wind. A dark figure broke through the storm. Tate. Seeing her, he stiffened and drew up to his full six-foot height. Formidable, he shouldered the door closed, frothed with white. He did not look happy to see her.

"Morning." He shouldered away to the potbellied stove in the sitting area and disregarded her entirely.

"Good morning." She spoke to his back as she skirted around the back of the couch, bringing the light with her. Awkward silence settled between them as she set the lamp on the round oak table. Why was she aware of every sound he made? The squeak of the stove's hinges, the crush of the shovel sinking into the coal, the rush and tumble of sizzling-hot ashes.

Would every morning be like this? With both of them wordlessly going about their work? Images long forgotten rose to the surface, memories that whispered and nudged her as she pulled the metal ring in the floor, lifted the door and descended the few steps into the cellar.

Faint light lit her way. The memories followed her as she lifted a bowl of eggs from a shelf and a slab of salt pork. She recalled her mother's voice calling the family to breakfast. Stockinged feet paraded across the braided rugs, little girls' voices sang out gleefully one on top of another, "I want pancakes" and "I do, too!" Chairs clattered, Pa's deep chuckle accompanied the flurry as he swept the littlest onto her chair and gave her plump cheek a kiss. "Sorry girls, but I get all the pancakes."

"No, Pa!" They would all squeal.

Smiling in memory, she tucked the butter bowl into the curve of one arm. The happy sounds followed her up the steps, fading to silence in the kitchen light. A few feet away, Tate hunkered down in front of the range, feeding the growing fire.

"Ought to be going good in a few minutes." He didn't look at her. He closed the door and grappled for his cane. "I'll make sure you have enough coal to last the day."

"Thank you." She set her load onto the table. "Should I wake Gertie?"

"Later. When the house is fully warm." He took the hod and disappeared into the lean-to.

How could she feel more alone than she'd ever been? She couldn't explain it. She squared her shoulders, gathering all the determination she could and chose a fry pan from the shelf. It clunked to a rest on the stovetop. There would be no pancakes this morning, she decided, haunted by her memories. She hadn't realized how deeply she'd wanted to find that past and recreate the joyfulness of her long-ago family.

Maybe I can do that for Gertie, she decided, lining a pan with slice after slice of salt pork. She would salvage what contentment she could for herself and give her new daughter the happiness and joy she deserved.

Her decision made it easier to crack the first egg and watch the white bubble when it met the hot pan. Footsteps and cane rapped closer. What about Tate? What did he deserve? She tapped a second egg against the lip of metal, watching a crack creep across the delicate shell.

Hopelessness clung to him like the cold draft from the lean-to as he sidled close to the stove with the load of coal. A living arrangement, that's what he wanted, as if she were nothing more than a cook and a maid, but she knew that wasn't right. That wasn't what he meant. Grim, he lowered the hod, nodded once to her. The apology poignant in his unguarded eyes made her thumb pierce the shell too hard. Egg innards tumbled into the pan in an untidy clump.

"I need to feed the horse and harness him, but I'll be back by the time you're finished cooking." No emotion carried in his tone, he sounded like a dead man walking as he gave a heavy sigh and turned away. "I'll take my meal with me. I've got a long work day ahead of me."

"I'll have it waiting for you when you're done at the barn." She reached for another egg from the bowl. Glancing over her shoulder, she watched him limp across the room, proud shoulders braced, powerful back straight, a man holding on to his dignity.

She knew what hardship could do. She knew how it felt to believe all the good in life was behind you. Was that what he thought? Didn't he know that you never knew what the good God had waiting for you somewhere up ahead? It was what she had learned holding out hope that her sisters would find her. She may not have found her first family, but she had the chance for another.

Aching filled her, a soreness that radiated from heart to rib, from soul to bone. She breathed out slowly, all she could manage with the fresh emotion lodged in her chest. She cracked the egg, placing the last runny white and bright yolk carefully into the pan. A little salt and pepper, and the salt pork was ready to turn. After giving everything a flip, she set last night's leftover biscuits in the oven to warm.

Cooking was all he would let her do for him. For regardless of her disappointment, he'd been honest with her. He was doing his best. This man would be her husband, and she would not stop caring.

What if he'd been too hard on her? The question troubled him as he fastened the harness buckles. Old Patches stood obediently, not complaining when a mean gust of wind hit. He wished he had some gentleness to spare for both the horse and the woman. The way she'd looked at him this morning twisted through him. He didn't like what he'd become.

"I won't be long, fella." He patted the gelding's neck and dreaded the few steps that would bring him to the house where Felicity was, going about her work in the kitchen, trying to hide her feelings. At least the woman was an open book, honest with her emotions. He appreciated it as he patted the horse's neck and headed toward the house.

It wasn't easy turning the doorknob, knowing she would be there. Fresh coffee and sizzling salt pork scented the air and he kept his gaze low to the floor so he wouldn't have to see that look. The one that told him she had come here looking for more than a convenient marriage, hoping for much more of a man than him. He didn't blame her. He steeled his spine, doing his best.

"I have your meal ready to go." Her step tapped toward him, a blue skirt swirled to a stop, and he had to look at her. Slender, soft hands held out a bundle wrapped in a dishtowel. His breakfast. He looked into her caring eyes, which were eager to please and his throat closed up. "I appreciate it."

"Here's a cup of coffee, although it's going to cool off fast in that cold." She spun around, moving like a waltz the few steps from door to table. Steam curled from the ironware cup she handed him along with a small pail. "And your lunch."

"My stomach will thank you come noon." Something jammed up tight in his chest. Probably another muscle spasm. He didn't know how to thank her well enough, so he smiled. "Maybe having a wife won't be such a bad thing, after all."

A smile blossomed across her face, glorious like the first rays of a new dawn rising. "I'll likely be a trial to you, but you were the one who advertised for a mail-order bride."

"So you're saying I get what I deserve?"

"Yes, and you will just have to accept the consequences." Little sparkles of gold flashed in her irises. "I shall try not to vex you too much."

"Too late for that," he quipped, meaning just the opposite and he suspected she knew that. Uncomfortable with the lightness, he turned away. At least the pinch of pain had vanished from the sweet curve of her rosebud mouth. Some of his guilt eased. Life had been hard for so long, he'd forgotten how kindness felt. He searched for it now in the empty places where his heart used to be and could not find it. Gruffly he turned, words tangling in his throat. Work waited, and he had one more person depending on him.

"Have a good day." Her words sailed behind him, undaunted by wind or snow, toasty in spite of the sub-zero temperature. Her brightness blinded him. It was too much to endure. He could not answer as his cane slipped on a patch of ice; he jerked to the right to keep his balance and pain slammed through his left side. The lunch pail crashed into the snow. He recoiled, wobbling on his feet, looking like a fool.

No, like a cripple. He hardened his defenses, making them unbreakable as he heard her skirts rustle behind him. The aftershock of pain lashed through him but he gritted his molars together and bent toward the pail. Slender fingers wrapped around the metal handle before he could. Felicity smelling of roses and butter plucked his lunch from the icy accumulation.

Humiliation gripped him, but it was nothing compared to his pride. He set his shoulders, unable to meet her gaze as he accepted the handle she offered him. Coat thrown on, unbuttoned, nothing on her hands or head. She would catch her death in this weather.

"Button up." He meant the words to be soft but they boomed out of him, sharp enough to cut glass. He wanted her to get back inside where she would be warm and snug, but when he opened his mouth nothing came out.

"I'll see you at supper time." Her fingers found his arm and squeezed gently, a silent communication of understanding. Was it possible she could sense what he meant? That she could hear what he hadn't been able to say?

He nodded, his throat entirely closed, unable to do more than limp away. Why didn't she mind the cane and the physical disability that made him less of a man? Out of the corner of his eye, he caught her good-bye wave, a dainty flutter of her finely sculpted fingers.

She really ought to get inside, he worried, troubled at his concern for her, touched by her kindness to him. No, it wasn't his heart thawing. Nothing could do that. As if in confirmation, the wind gusted, the snowfall thickened and all he could see was her faint outline against the glow falling through the doorway. That image stayed with him all day long.

"What is your pa going to think?" Felicity climbed off the chair and dragged it away from the sitting-area window. Her back ached slightly from all the heavy lifting and her muscles burned pleasantly from the day of work.

"He's gonna love it." Gertie clasped her hands together, pure sweetness. "It's the prettiest home ever."

"I'm glad you think so and I agree." She couldn't help reaching out to the child and brushing blond bangs from dazzling eyes. "It's the only real home I've had in a long time."

"Because your ma and pa died." Gertie nodded with sympathy, her forehead furrowing with thought. "I remember that from your letters. Do you know what?"

"What?" She gave one twin braid a loving tug.

"It's mine, too. There was a boardinghouse and before that a room above the tannery." Gertie heaved out a painful sigh, as if lost in tough memories. "After that Aunt Ingrid found me, and I lived with her over the feed store. That's where Pa's staying now. I was real glad she came for me."

"I'm glad, too." The poor child. She dropped to her knees, Gertie's misery palpable. Would it be better to change the subject? Why hadn't she been with Tate? "I'm glad you're right here with your pa and with me."

"Me, too." Gertie rubbed her eyes with the back of her hand. "I didn't like the orphanage. Not at all. Did you like it there?"

"No." Shock twisted her in half until she crumpled inside. Gertie had been a ward of the territory? She thought of Tate's cane and disability, the one he fought hard to hide. Had he been unable to take care of her? How had he been injured? Questions itched on her tongue longing to be asked but she held them back.

Poor Gertie. She pulled the child to her, breathed in her little-girl scent sweet like Christmas cookies and honey soap, and gave thanks that God had brought her back together with her family, with her father.

Lord, I know why You brought me here. She raised the thought in prayer. Never would she have guessed that her past and Gertie's were similar.

"When I was a little girl and wanted cheering up, my ma would make chipped beef on toast. I don't know if you would like it—"

"Oh, it's one of my favorites." Gertie sniffled,

straightened her shoulders and her throat worked, as if struggling to put her sadness behind her.

"Then it's settled. I'm fixing you a special supper. Here's hoping your pa likes it, too." Grief for the child snuck inside her, stubbornly refusing to let go. Vowing to be all that Gertie needed, she brushed away a single tear from those satin cheeks. "Is Merry still napping? Or does she want to watch me make supper, too?"

"I'll go get her." Gertie slipped away, the past trailing her like smoke. The hardship that had touched this family was worse than she'd realized. And poor Tate, separated from his daughter. He had to have been torn apart.

Sunset squeezed the daylight from the sky, drawing shadows into the cheerful room. Felicity lit the lamp and turned up the wick so that the golden glow shone on the calico tablecloth and shimmered on the curtains at the window. Satisfaction filled her as she studied her handiwork. The colorful braid rugs brought out the sheen of the wood floor. The wicker basket and quilted wall hanging she'd pieced cheered up the space between the windows. She'd spun dreams stitching the things for the home she would have one day.

That day was here. She felt heaven's touch like a comforting weight on her shoulders. A girl's dreams might not turn out the way she'd envisioned, but she had nearly everything she'd wished for. A little girl who shared her heart, who was a kindred soul. A home to fill with love. A place and people who needed her. This is what she had longed for. This was her answered prayer. Just one thing was missing.

The door swung open to reveal a snow-covered man in a shabby black coat. Tate. He had to be terribly cold out in the weather all day. She plucked the cozy off the teapot and checked it. Yes, still hot.

What if he was wrong and love could grow between them?

"Come in," she called. "Warm up. I'll bring you something to drink."

Had he heard her? She couldn't tell. His hat brim shaded his face, hiding his reaction as he surveyed the far side of the room. Was he regretting having a woman in charge of his house? Or perhaps he didn't have heart enough to care. He merely shrugged, dusted off the snow, hung up his things and limped heavily to the sofa. Brutal cold chased the warmth from the air, the storm outside was worsening.

"Thank you." He kept his head down, ignoring her as she slid the steaming sweetened tea onto the scarred end table. Strain carved into his square jaw. Perhaps the bitter cold pained his bad leg. She suspected he would not admit it if she asked.

"You're not here to wait on me." He glared up at her but beyond the severe set of his handsome features lurked something more. Something substantial and real.

"I'm here for Gertie, I know." Not once had he commented on all the lace and the predominantly pink floral fabrics. She was sure it was appreciation she saw in the bleak blue depths of his eyes as she drifted to the kitchen. Probably not appreciation over all the pink, but at least he appeared to approve.

"Pa! Don't you just love everything?" The girl dashed into his arms with Merry tucked in hers. "Felicity had it all in her trunk."

"That's why it was so heavy." Humor lingered at the edges of his words. Just a hint, but enough to make a smile stretch her face as she grabbed the cutting board from its shelf.

"She sewed everything." Gertie snuggled Merry to her and hopped onto the couch. "She made some of it before she knew me. But this she did after."

Father and daughter bent together to study the afghan on the back cushion. Light pink flowers on a background of leaf-green and snow-white. Gertie ran her forefinger across a puffy raised petal. Side by side, Felicity could see the resemblance. Where Gertie's features were delicate and sweet, father and daughter shared the same shape eyes, high cheekbones and full jaw.

"And look at the rug. It's one big braid. So's the one under the table." Gertie disappeared from sight, presumably on the floor. "She got scraps for free from her work. Isn't that right, Felicity?"

"Absolutely." She uncovered the roast, talking as she worked. "I made all sorts of things with those scraps. Quilts, wall hangings, even Merry. But with her, I used only the very best pieces."

"That's why she's so beautiful." Gertie studied the doll cradled in her arm and kissed the cloth forehead the way a real mother would.

Sweet. But it was Tate's reaction that hit her in the heart. His jaw dropped. His eyes squeezed shut. He looked like a man on the edge of losing his iron control. Tendons stood out in his neck. Tension snapped along his jaw line. Callused hands fisted as if it took all his strength to hold back his emotions. He swallowed hard. When he opened his eyes they were glassy. Emotion had won.

"Best get to some of the work waiting outside." He cleared his throat but his voice wasn't as hollow or as hard. He rose up to his six-foot-plus height, cloaked in his secrets except for the devotion written on his face.

He smoothed one rough hand tenderly against the side of Gertie's face briefly, just for that moment he was no longer bleak. But it returned to wrap around him like the shadows, the weight of failure and loss and adversity, things that were a mystery to her as she watched him head for the door.

"How long until we eat?" He threw the question her way, busy with his coat.

"Thirty minutes or so." She wanted to go to him, to lay her hand on the immense plane of his shoulder, to comfort him. But her feet stayed rooted in place, knowing he would refuse her. "I can wait longer if you wish."

"Thirty minutes will be fine." He bit out the words, meaning to be gruff but she heard something else. "I'll be back."

"And I will have supper hot and waiting."

He stiffened. For one moment he did not move. He did not seem to breathe. Shadows gathered around him like nightfall setting in. Despair lived deep inside the man, that was why he kept his back to her hiding what he didn't want her to see. Well, she knew something about broken hearts. No matter how shattered, the human heart yearned to be loved. Tate shouldered out the door with a thump of his cane, a flutter of blue scarf and the creak of hinges closing, a great hulking darkness.

She'd never seen anyone who needed love more.

Chapter Seven

"So you are the lady Gertie has been telling me all about." Reverend Hadly squeezed her hand as if he were meeting a long-lost friend. "Wonderful to meet you, Felicity."

"It's a pleasure to meet you. I loved your sermon." The sanctuary was crowded after the service, full of people engaged in conversations or waiting to speak with their minister. "I hear you are the man who will be marrying us."

Beside her, Gertie hopped up and down. Tate cleared his throat. He stood tall, trying his best not to lean heavily on his cane. She'd thought him closed off before but she barely recognized this statue of a man with chin set, spine straight and guards up.

"That I am." The reverend's compassionate brown eyes studied Tate before flicking over to her. "I have plenty of time before the Christmas Eve service. With the church lit up, it will be a lovely ceremony."

"I'm getting a new dress," Gertie chimed in. "Felicity and I are going to start making it after we get home."

"You must be excited." Reverend Hadly's sympathy spoke volumes, easy to read his happiness for the child and his concern for the man as he clapped Tate on the shoulder. "Congratulations again. God is giving you a new chance, Tate. I'm happy for all of you."

Strain bunched along Tate's jawline, his only reaction as he took a step forward. Whatever happened, the minister knew of the family's hardships and knew them well. True sympathy shone from brown eyes, stirring the same within her.

"Good day to you, Hadly." Tate's cane thumped on the floor, betraying his strain. Was it being in church that troubled him? Or surrounded by so many people? When Gertie's hand crept into hers, realization sifted over her like the quietly falling snow. She blinked against the airy flakes flying into her face as she tapped down the front steps.

Of course. Why hadn't she thought of it before? This was Tate's home church. He had attended here with his wife, when his family was whole. Had her funeral been performed in this church? Gertie's christening? His wedding?

"Oh, I pity that woman," a pitched whisper carried her way. She felt watched.

She was. A trio of women in their Sunday best stared at her as if she were a window display in a shop. Should she smile? Greet them? What poor woman in need of pity were they talking about?

"Come on." Gertie's hand in hers tugged hard. "Where's Aunt Ing?"

"Here I am." Ingrid appeared, breathless. She deftly blocked the trio of women with a tight smile. "We'll let the men get the horses. Don't you adore our reverend?"

"Yes, he is the nicest man." She swallowed hard, realizing the women were still staring. Ingrid hadn't blocked them entirely. Felicity took a careful step in the snow. Surely those women didn't feel sorry for *her?*

Tate trudged diagonally away from them toward the horse, a powerful force radiating manliness and might. Black hat, black coat, black trousers, he was a silhouette against the stretch of white snow, achingly alone. His left leg might drag a bit, but how could anyone see the disability and not the man? The caring within her strengthened until no force could break it.

"We are blessed in our reverend," Ingrid went on talking. "He leads our Bible Study on Saturdays. You could come along with me and see what it's like, if you're interested."

"Yes. Absolutely."

"Wonderful. I can't wait to introduce you around. Oh, this is going to be so fun." Ingrid reached the edge of the yard, where oldest brother, Devin, waited in the feed store's rough-hewn wooden sled. A pair of study horses swished their tails, patiently waiting while Ingrid hugged first Gertie, and then Felicity goodbye.

I'm going to love having a sister again, she thought, waving as the sled pulled away. Joy crept into her, making the day bright and so did the pressure of the small hand tucked in her own. Now that she'd discussed the wedding ceremony with the minister, nerves popped in her stomach. The good sort of nerves, the same she'd felt when she'd held Gertie's first letter or stood on the platform waiting to board the westbound train with Tate's ticket clenched in her fist.

A ticket that must have been very difficult to afford. The old pinto nosed into the spot Devin's sled had vacated, drawing Tate and the wagon box to a stop in front of her. His scarf did bring out the incredible shade of his eyes. Maybe it was a trick of the gray daylight or the power of her enduring wish, but his gaze gentled when he looked at her. The craggy stone of his face softened. Just for one brief moment.

Just for her.

"Pa, are you gonna stay home today?" Gertie hopped onto the seat. Tate set down the reins to help her.

"You know I have work to do." He held out his hand, palm up, turning into a statue of a man again with feelings hidden and heart barricaded.

Maybe it had been the light, after all. Disappointment crept in but she lifted her chin, refusing to let it show. She laid her bare fingertips on his broad palm, barely touching him as she stepped onto the running board. "You deliver on Sundays?"

"No, but it's a good time to go over the equipment. To keep everything running smoothly." He gathered the reins, glancing over his shoulder to check for traffic. A jam of horses and sleighs waited on the street, so with a sigh he loosened the reins, resigned to wait. "After hours, when I'm done with any last-minute deliveries for the store, I run loads for a local teamster."

He worked two jobs? So that's how he paid for her train ticket. That explained why he left in the evenings after supper. What else didn't she know about him? The bulk of it could fill her hope chest to overflowing.

Finally the horses and vehicles thinned, and with a snap of the reins, Patches pulled them forward. The runners bumped over ruts in the road and snow swirled playfully into her eyes. Tate sat straight and tall in the seat, more handsome than he'd ever been to her. What a blessing he was. God had shown great a kindness in leading her to him. Affection bloomed like a rare rose in winter, gently and sweetly and budding with hope. Surely her caring could make a difference.

"Gertie—" she leaned close to the girl, taking care that her whisper would not carry "—what is your pa's favorite meal?"

"Chicken and dumplings," she whispered back. Gossamer curls framed her button face. "Are you gonna make it for him?"

"It happens to be my specialty."

The rig had seen better days five years ago. On his back beneath the wagon box, Tate gave the wrench a good hard twist. Lantern light cast orange flickers across the wood section of the frame he'd just replaced, but the mountings were solid. He set down the wrench and gave them a test. Everything held and he sighed with relief. That was one thing crossed off his list. He inched his way, checking stress points as he went until he'd cleared the frame and sat up behind the runners.

"That ought to hold for the rest of the winter," he told the gelding who eyed him over the top of his stall. "At least we'll hope so."

Patches nickered in agreement, earning a nose rub. The old fellow was a good horse. Tate was grateful for the animal's gentle and amiable spirit. The work days were long but the gelding never complained.

"Felicity! Look!" Gertie's high words rang through the yard like a merry bell. He caught sight of her dashing down the steps bundled up well against the cold. A navy scarf protected her neck from the wind and trailed down her back, fringe waving in the wind. Beige gloves, also far too big, protected her hands as she dashed into the yard's deep snow. Her giggles lifted in the air, the sound most precious to him.

He had Felicity to thank for that. His chest cinched tight. How he'd gotten so lucky, he didn't know. He suspected luck had nothing to do with it. He dropped the wrench into the tool box and leaned against the doorway. He drank in the sight of his daughter throwing out her arms and spinning with the wind.

"Look, Felicity! I'm twirling like a snowflake."

"Not yet, you're not!" The woman moved like a waltz, one lilting step after another, too graceful to touch the ground for long. She scooped up the little girl and lifted her high in the air. Gertie squealed, coming back down to wrap her arms around Felicity's neck. They spun together, the woman going faster and faster until they were a flutter of motion, of gold hair and swirling skirts and openhearted laughter.

He watched until they blurred. Only then did he turn away, blinking hard against the burn behind his eyes. Dumb snow. Getting in his eyes like that. He swaggered over to the wagon bed and hunkered down, needing to check the boards for wear.

He knew the exact moment when the laughter stopped. He didn't look up, although he heard everything. Gertie flopping into the snow and flapping to make an angel, Felicity's praise, the crunch of one pair of shoes coming closer. He set his jaw, unprepared to see the woman. A man ought to be safe in his own barn.

"Whew, I'm out of breath." She tumbled in, bringing the echoes of merriment with her. "I haven't played in the snow like that since, well, I can't exactly remember when. Brrr. You must be freezing in this weather."

"I'm used to it." Gratitude clogged in his throat made the words curt and coarser than he meant. He forced his gaze on the boards and *only* on the boards. Muscles twisted behind his sternum, making it hard to concentrate.

"You've been working out here most of the afternoon." She padded closer and the muscles in his chest snapped tight, near to breaking. The cutting board came into sight, a makeshift tray. "I thought you might like some hot tea and biscuits. I melted butter and honey on them. Just how you like it."

He wasn't prepared for this. The hammer in his grip wobbled. The knot in his throat expanded. "That is good of you, Felicity. You didn't need to do this."

"I wanted to." Undaunted by his growly tone, she set the tray on the wagon bed in front of him. Her hands were bare, for she'd given Gertie her gloves. "I can't have you freezing solid out here like an icicle. Who would I marry then?"

"I imagine any number of bachelors would line up to have you."

"So you *are* capable of being charming. I suspected it." She leaned her elbows against the bed's rail, propping her chin on one hand. Like a storybook princess, melting snowflakes winked in her hair, a tiara of diamonds. "Trust me, there isn't a single bachelor lined up to marry me. Not counting you, of course."

Talk about charming. He found himself leaning in closer, just a bit, taking in the little things about her he'd never let himself notice before. A chip of a dimple on the right side of her smile, the adorable way she tipped her head slightly to the left, the cute furrow above the bridge of her nose. Not that he could be charmed, but anyone would notice her loveliness. He couldn't believe she'd been on her own for so long. "There was never anyone for you?"

"Not a single beau." She dimmed, and he was sorry he'd asked. She gave a little shoulder shrug. "I always feared there was something about me. Maybe some inability to be loved that men could sense left over from being raised without family ties. Maybe loneliness is like a flaw men can spot and so shy away from."

"More than likely you scared off every man who looked your way." He blushed, realizing he hadn't thought the words, but said them aloud. They hovered in the air, too late to snatch back.

"Oh, because of my flaw, you mean, being so lonely?" She shook her head, scattering diamonds that fell to become melting snowflakes once again.

"Yes. No." He didn't know what he meant. The woman scattered his thoughts, too. "Because you are lovely in every way."

"If I get compliments like that, I should bring you tea more often." Self-conscious, she handed him the steaming cup. Clearly she didn't believe him. "Don't you have any gloves?"

"Work gloves. I wear them only when I need to. Have to make them last." He wrapped his hands across the mug, drawing the warmth into his skin. The aroma of strong tea and generous honey curled into the air. He breathed it in, letting it warm him.

"Where are they?"

"The gloves? On the shelf above the bridle hook." He should tell her to leave them alone. He ought to order her out of his barn, but he didn't have the will to force her away.

Through the frame of the open door, his daughter hopped up to inspect her work, her back covered in snow. Apparently satisfied, she chose another spot and fell backward, arms outstretched. A much different child from the sad, withdrawn shadow she'd been when he'd come home from prison. He squeezed his eyes shut, willing the agony down.

"Sorry, but I'm confiscating these." Felicity drew his attention. Her color brought life to the dimness where the lantern refused to reach. Her skirts swirled, a swatch of blue beneath the hem of her coat, the dainty pad of her steps tapped closer. Patches nickered low in his throat, perhaps hoping she would head his way.

"They are beginning to wear, but I can definitely mend them." Determined, she leaned against the tailgate, tucking his gloves into her pockets. "Don't give me that look. I love to fix things. It's another fault of mine."

"Your faults are starting to add up." Where the quip came from, he couldn't say. "Maybe I should rethink the proposal."

"Sure, go ahead. A woman's flaws may be numerous, but they are never as many as a man's." Demure humor bronzed the gold flecks in her irises. She wanted to make him laugh.

"That may be." She nearly succeeded. The strange lurch of a chuckle caught in his windpipe. Surprised, he shook his head. He'd almost laughed. Her humor was gentle, her true meaning hid beneath the words and he wondered exactly what she saw in him. Maybe she had no clue what his flaws were. He lifted the cup and drank, letting the hot sweetness slide across his tongue and wash his throat.

"Can I ask you something?" She broke the silence sounding somber. Sounding caring. *Caring?* He could weed out that one untrustworthy emotion, refusing to be hooked by it. When he didn't answer, she continued on. "How did you hurt your leg?"

Her question struck like a blow. He heard the air rush out of his lungs. Pain streaked to his soul. This discussion was inevitable. She deserved to know the truth about the man she intended to marry. He glanced over her shoulder to the child making angels in the snow.

"Maybe I shouldn't have asked." Apology polished her words, made them sweet and translucent to show her true concern beneath.

"You have the right. I'm debating the best way to tell you." He swallowed hard. Where did he start? How did he find the words? He barricaded his chest so not one emotion could escape. "I was nearly beaten to death on my own property by men who are in prison now."

"How horrible." Sympathy and fondness twined together and he'd never heard emotion so pure. "Tate, I'm sorry that happened to you. That's awful. Was this at the feed store?"

"No. My father owned the place at that time, before his illness. It happened at my ranch." Time spun backward. He could feel the December snow crackle against his cheek as his face slammed into the ground. Although he tried to stop it, he recalled the hammer-like blow of a boot bashing pain through his skull. He swallowed hard, trying to stop the memories of masked men towering high above him. "First they wanted a couple of my horses. With a knife to my throat, I let them take the team. Then they marched me from the barn to my house, wanting what money I had on hand. When they put the knife to my wife Lolly's throat, I pulled the rock out of the chimney and handed them our entire savings."

"Those terrible men. Was the sheriff able to arrest them right away?"

"The man with the knife *was* the sheriff. He didn't bother with a bandanna. Dobbs said if I told anyone I would regret it." Tension rippled along his jaw and stood out in his neck. "I kept silent for a while. Lolly was afraid of what would happen. Those same masked men visited other farms and other businesses over time. Folks recognized my horses and figured I was one of those men. It was all rumor and assumption, but it was hard to take."

"Of course. That was terribly unfair. How could you stomach it?"

"One day I couldn't take it anymore. I visited the telegraph office to send word to the governor about what was happening. Turns out one of the operators was working for Dobbs. I received another visit in the middle of the night. I was yanked out of bed, kicked through the house and beaten on my front lawn. Dobbs arrested me for the crimes he and his men committed and demanded the deed to my land for good measure."

"You were falsely arrested?"

"Yes and when the truth came to light, immediately released." He sat on the back of the wagon bed, as mighty as a warrior, drawing in the shadows like air. "A lot of folks in this town still suspect I was guilty.

I broke most of the bones on my left side in that beating, and the territory didn't spend a lot on a doctor to put me back together when I was in jail."

"You should have been treated better." Rips gathered along the seams of her heart, slowly tearing deeper. No wonder. How had his spirit survived that level of cruelty? "Was that when Gertie was in an orphanage?"

"You know about that?" He gaze lashed hers, hard and fraught with agony.

"She told me."

"Her mother cut off all connection to me. I can still hear her words when I was being beaten and bleeding so hard I couldn't see for the blood streaming into my eyes. Lolly's last words were that I deserved what I got. She was mad at me for standing up against Dobbs. I put her and Gertie in jeopardy. She said that I had done that to myself and she would never forgive me. She took off. She ran off hoping for a new start."

"She took Gertie? She never wrote to tell you? She didn't care what happened to you?"

"Ingrid spent months looking for her. By the time she did Lolly had died of pneumonia—she always was frail—and Gertie wound up in a bad place. Not like the home you were in." His face twisted. "If Ingrid hadn't rescued her…"

He said nothing more. His pain palpable on the breeze blew into her soul.

What could she do to comfort him and to soothe away that depth of suffering? She reached across the distance between them. When her hand settled on his forearm, he stiffened. The tension bunched in his jaw and corded in his neck became so tight, it looked able to break bone. He did not move away.

"You tried to do the right thing. I admire you for that." She sensed he needed to hear it but it was also the truth. He shrugged, a brief lift of his dependable shoulders, discounting her. But his granite features winced once, a show of emotion. Encouraged, she inched a little closer along the tailgate. "Gertie is all right now. Look at her."

Apparently that was the right thing to say. Relieved, she watched as Tate focused on his daughter, who had bounced up to study her work in the snow. The last veil of snowflakes waltzed from sky to earth and danced around her like a ballet and the golden-haired girl clasped her hands together, pleased with the angel impressions in the sugar-pure snow.

"Yes, she's better now," he agreed. Beneath her fingertips, his tensed muscles relaxed through his soft flannel sleeve. "Thanks to you."

"I'm not the one who works two jobs to provide for her."

"It won't always be this way." His throat worked, struggling with emotions she could only guess at. "The economy will turn around and Devin's store will be running at a profit again. I'll get back on my feet financially. I promise to buy you and Gertie a nice house, one fit for all that frilly frippery you women like to make."

"I can make the frippery less frilly next time. I don't have to use so much pink."

"I don't mind. I spent a lot of tough nights in a dark, icy jail cell with no comforts. Not one. It's been a long time since a house has felt like a home." He said nothing more because his chest felt ready to explode. The vacant spot where his heart used to be hurt as if it had been beaten.

"I'm glad I could do that for you, give you a home again. I need one, too." Her fingertips lifted away from his, but distance could not break the connection forged between them. She pushed away from the tailgate, as cheerful as the sunshine peeking between dying clouds. "I'll be back soon. I'm going to meet the next-door neighbors."

"The Tillys aren't the friendliest sort."

"No, but they have a chicken house and I have four doilies to trade." Her chip of a dimple dug in next to the soft curve of her rosebud mouth. She was grace and goodness sailing away from him. She was everything he'd stopped believing in long ago.

He shook his head as she disappeared from his sight. The poor neighbors. They didn't have a chance. Who could say no to her? He took another swallow of tea. It had cooled down enough not to burn his tongue.

"Pa! Come look." Gertie spun in place, catching the last of the snowflakes on the palms of her too-big gloves. "I made three snow angels. A pa, a ma and a little girl. A family."

As he reached for his cane and pushed to his feet, those words echoed within him. *A family.* Was that why Gertie had wanted a mother so much? His bad knee wobbled but he kept on going, determined to give his daughter the attention and praise she needed, but inside, he'd turned to stone. He'd given her and Felicity all he could. All he had.

He had nothing left within him, and for good reason. His heart broke when his wife turned away from him. His faith shattered when he'd stood in front of a judge listening to Dobbs's men lie to cover their own crimes. Days and nights in the hardest prison in the territory smothered his soul. He had only pieces to offer, and what good was that?

Snow crunched beneath his boots and the last snowflake fell, brushing his cheek. The bitter cold didn't touch him as he trudged to a stop beside his daughter. His precious girl.

"That's a fine family." The words scratched against the inside of his tightening throat. Gertie's hand crept into his and he wished he had some tenderness to show her. He wished he could give her the family she wanted and Felicity the loving husband she'd come looking for. He feared what would happened if he couldn't.

Chapter Eight

Dear Eleanor,
I hope this finds you well and settled in Dry Creek. I would have written sooner, but I hadn't imagined there would be so much to do. I've unpacked all my hope chest items and Tate accepted every change I made. He's a man wounded by life but I pray God's love will heal him. Gertie and I are two peas in a pod. She loved the doll, just as you predicted. Whew.

Felicity lifted her pen from the paper and dipped it into the ink bottle, wondering what more to say. The house echoed around her, lonely with Gertie at school but that would soon be fixed. The clock on the mantel ticked closer to three o'clock, when she would leave for the schoolhouse. She blotted off the excess ink and began to write again.

What about you? I saw a kindly couple greet you when you disembarked. Are they your new

*in-laws? What about your husband-to-be? I
noticed he wasn't there to meet your train. Is
everything all right? I worry for you, Eleanor,
and I'm praying for you. With all your hardships, you deserve a good husband and a loving
future. I hope this Christmas finds you happily
married. All my love,
Felicity*

She thought of her friend. God had brought them
together on the train, two mail-order brides. *Lord,
please watch over Eleanor and help us to both find
our happily ever afters.*

The tick of the clock was the only answer, reminding her to hurry. She twisted the ink bottle lid tight,
folded her letter and slipped it into the envelope. She
gave one final glance around the living room, turned
down the damper on the potbelly stove and slipped
into her coat.

The house felt cozy as she headed to the door. Last
night's contentment lingered in the room, filling her
with hope. She could still see Tate by the fire repairing
a harness in the lamplight, while Gertie sat near his feet
playing tea party with Merry. Tate might have wanted
a convenient marriage, but the contentment in the air
when they were all together felt like much more.

Please, let it be, she wished.

She tumbled through the door, aglow with memories. Already her dream was coming true. They were
almost a family. Brisk air knifed through her layers of
wool and flannel, but nothing could dampen her optimism. Not one thing.

"Hello there, pretty lady." A familiar baritone cut into her thoughts. "Can I offer you a ride?"

"Tate!" She whirled, stunned to see him gazing at her from beneath the low slant of his hat brim. He looked good with the wind ruffling his hair, so incredibly good. A welcoming grin hinted in the corners of his mouth, where the promise of a dimple lived. Could she help it if her feelings soared? "I didn't even hear Patches."

"You were lost in thought?" he guessed, nodding as if that didn't surprise him. He reached across the span of the seat to take her hand. "I thought so. I called your name twice—no response."

The contact of his hand to hers sent a stronger surge of caring through her. She swallowed hard, clearing her throat, to keep her affection for him out of her voice. "Are you off to make a round of deliveries?"

"Yes. This is my last route for the day." He leaned forward, offering his assistance as she stepped from street to running board. "The gloves are holding up great. Thanks for mending them. You did wonders."

"It was easy to do. I see your coat is next."

"I've noticed you've already taken a needle to my denims and my shirts."

"Guilty." She searched his gaze for the slightest sigh of affection and found none. *I'm not disappointed,* she thought, but she was. Yesterday's closeness had affected her, but apparently not him. He seemed formidable as he snapped the reins. Patches lunged forward, glad to keep moving in the cold air. "We haven't talked about Christmas presents for Gertie."

"I've decided to make her a doll cradle. Wish I could afford to buy her one, but it's all Ingrid, Devin and I can do to scrape up funds for the wood and paint." He drew up taller, as if bracing himself, obviously uncomfortable and struggling not to be.

Please, she thought. *Just care about me a little.* After what he'd been through, love would take time coming back into his heart, but it had to come. She could already see the changes in the quiet moments, in the edges of his smile and in the hidden gentleness he showed her. Those things gave her hope.

"She had her doll taken from her when she arrived at the orphanage." The softness was a hint in the hard pools of his eyes, a clue to the man beneath. "It was her only comfort, the only thing she had left of her own."

"Poor Gertie. She'd lost her mother and her father, everything she knew. That had to have been the last straw."

"It was. When I saw that doll..." His throat worked. "Well, you'll just never know how much I appreciate you."

Appreciation. That was a step. Already the distance between them began to fade. Definitely a positive sign. "I also sewed an entire wardrobe of clothes to go with the doll."

"And you saved that for Christmas?"

"Yes. I had the dearest time designing and sewing those clothes. I would sit in my room in the evenings and, with every stitch, know I was sewing for my daughter. Hoping that she would adore the little clothes as much as I loved making them."

"She will." A faint curve inched up the corners of his chiseled mouth. He blinked hard, possibly against the cold breeze that hurled against them when Patches turned onto Main. "Looks like she'll get a good Christmas, after all."

"Yes, but there is something missing. You must see a lot of trees when you're out on deliveries." She gestured toward the town street. "Okay, not here exactly, but when you drive out of town. There has to be a tree somewhere you could chop down and bring home to decorate."

"I'll borrow Devin's ax in case I see one somewhere." He shook his head. Why he was agreeing he didn't know. He tried to tell himself it was for Gertie. Imagine her eyes on Christmas morning with her doll cradle and clothes beneath green boughs waiting just for her. Why, she would like that, and he figured Felicity would, too.

"Excellent. I'll get a spot picked out in the sitting area for it." Pleasure drew pink in her cheeks and teased out the gold accents in her eyes.

He ought to be careful. An unsuspecting man could get lost in those depths. She tilted her head slightly to one side and gossamer wisps swept against the curve of her face. Her beautiful face.

He swallowed hard. Nuances of emotion lingered inside him, ghosts of what he was once able to feel. Troubled by it, he focused all his attention on the road and on the reins in his hands. Patches trotted through the busiest part of town and turned onto the intersecting street. The schoolhouse rose into sight. The emotion remained, like smoke disbursing in a wind, fading into nothingness again.

"I want Christmas to be the best we can make it." She turned toward him in the seat. "Last year Gertie spent Christmas in the orphanage, didn't she?"

"Yep." The words felt wrung out of him. He knew what she would be saying next. He bowed his head, bracing for it.

"You were in jail."

He gritted his teeth so tight, his molars hurt. All he could manage was a nod. It was important to keep all his pain deeply buried so he wouldn't feel it. His hand crept over to cover hers. Not that he needed her comfort or the connection of her understanding.

Fine. He did.

"I'll see you when you get home tonight." Her fingers clung to his as she eased off the seat. "I'm making a special supper."

"And maybe those biscuits of yours?"

"I'm not telling." She sank into the snow. "I'm leaving it a mystery. You'll have to wait to find out."

"I know what you're doing. Gertie is telling you my favorite meals so you can make them." He didn't let go of her. His grip felt unbreakable, as unreadable as his gaze.

"As far as I can tell, you seem to like what I've been cooking."

"I wasn't complaining. Just trying to figure you out."

"Good luck with that."

They chuckled together for a cozy moment. His

gentleness shone warmth into his hard gaze, showing the real man beneath. Just a glimpse, before the walls snapped up and blocked her out.

But she'd seen the core of him. She wasn't wrong. He cared more than he could admit. She hid her affection beneath a quick smile. She hated letting go of him.

"I'd like to stay," he said. "See Gertie. Take the two of you home, but I have deliveries to make."

"I have an errand, anyway." The wind whipped up between them, nudging her backward a step. "Gertie promised to show me where the post office is."

"Do you need money for a stamp?"

"No, I already have one." She patted her coat pocket. "I brought it with me. Are you going to wait to see Gertie?"

"I can't. I'd best get going." The lean line of his mouth upturned into a small smile as he tipped his hat to her. "I'll see you tonight for the mystery supper."

"Beware because it could be anything." Beef stew, but leaving him in suspense widened his smile into a full grin. Stunning. That was the only word that came to mind. She went up on tiptoes, drawn to him, wanting to hold on as he began to go. Patches stepped forward, ears pricked, necked arched. The runners squeaked on the snow.

"I'll eat anything you cook as long as you make those biscuits with it." A wink, a tip of his hat but no warmth chased the shadows from his gaze. No love lit him as he rode away. Long streaks of light cut around him, stealing him from her sight.

But there was a chance. She saw it.

Please watch over him, Lord, she prayed in the chilly sunshine. *Please heal his heart.*

The school bell rang, drawing her attention back to the world around her. The doors flew open, noise and chaos erupted and children dashed down the steps. Shouts rang against the bright blue sky, the sounds of freedom and childhood.

"Felicity!" Gertie broke away from the steps, alone. She carried her schoolbooks tucked in the crook of her arm and swung her lunch pail with her free hand. She dashed through the snow. "Guess what?"

"What?"

"I got every spelling word right. I got the best score!"

"You did? Wonderful job. I'm so proud of you. You are such a smart girl." She knelt to draw the child into her arms. The love within her built with each breath, each moment, each smile. Love not just for Gertie.

When she glanced down the road, Tate was simply a dark speck against the stretching white of the high-winter prairie. *Please love me,* she wished. *Please.*

What he was doing chopping down a tree, he didn't know. He was a fool, that's what, taking time out of his evening when he ought to be heading back to town and checking with Emmett Simms. If there was any extra hauling work to be done, then he ought to be imagining that and not the joy on Felicity's face when she caught sight of this fir.

Disappointed, that's what he was. He was smarter than this. So why didn't he stop chopping?

Good question. A question he didn't want to answer

or he would have to admit something he didn't want to face. His relationship with the woman was headed toward certain disaster and he hadn't even married her yet. All it took was one plea on her gentle face and here he was, chopping.

He swung the ax one more time, pitching it in a slant so the tree would tip straight and clean. The blade dug in and the scrubby fir bounced to a rest on the drifted snow, branches flung out, trembling from the impact.

The tree wasn't much, hardly six feet, but it was the largest he'd come across on unclaimed land. He pictured delight tracing pink across Felicity's face when she spotted him driving up with this and his chest knotted tight.

The fir slid behind him as he plunged through thigh-high drifts. Patches watched from the road, seeming to shake his head in disbelief. The tangible weight of his failings rested like an anvil on his sternum, painful with each breath, each step, and when he hefted the tree into the wagon box.

This was a bad idea, he thought as he tied the tree in tight. The idea seemed even worse as he settled on the seat and took up the reins. The last Christmas tree he'd had was before Dobbs and his men had ruined his life. He'd gathered around that tree with his wife beside him, thinking that all loves lasted. He'd watched Gertie's delight as she'd unwrapped the china doll from beneath a candlelit tree. His contented world was crushed to bits three days later.

If a man kept his hopes low, they couldn't be taken

away from him. As he snapped the reins, fear gnawed inside him. Was he walking on hazardous ground? He would be smart to figure out how to say no to Felicity. That was why he'd lost the argument with himself and stopped to cut the tree. That was why he was heading home with the smell of fresh-cut pine accompanying him.

Felicity. He shook his head. What was he going to do? She had agreed to a marriage of convenience, but she hoped for more. Anyone could see the plea in her eyes, longing to be loved. He had to marry her. Gertie couldn't take it if he changed his mind and sent Felicity away.

He couldn't take it.

The house came into sight. Lamplight shining on the other side of pink curtains cast a rosy glow onto the glass. Home. She had done a good job of that. The welcoming light drew him into the yard. When Patches clomped to a stop outside the door, a section of curtain pulled back. Gertie's dear face beamed out at him. No, he couldn't do that to his little girl.

The door flung open, spilling light and a child onto the porch.

"Pa!" Gertie gaped, hands clasped, disbelieving. "Is that a *tree?* A *real* Christmas tree?"

"It could be." He set down the reins. "Let's go take a look."

"Oh, Papa." She flew down the steps in a swirl of gingham, wool and Felicity's gloves. "It is! I can't believe it. This really is going to be a *real* Christmas."

"That's what I promised you, little one." He leaned

heavily on his cane. "We're together again. We'll be together for every Christmas to come, you and me."

"And Felicity," Gertie added. That button face—it stopped him in his tracks. It outshone the stars above. The misery that had haunted her from her mother's death and her stay at the orphanage melted away like shadows before a high-noon sun. Just brightness and glory remained.

No, he had to go forward with this marriage. There was no going back. Felicity and Gertie belonged together, two peas in a pod.

"Felicity! Come see what Pa brought," Gertie hollered, ruffling the green tip of a feathery evergreen bough and causing the rich tree scent to rise on the wind. "It's just the best surprise. I think God heard my prayers, Pa. He finally heard."

He knew it wasn't the tree she meant. Shame rushed through him for all the ways he'd failed her. He'd done his best fighting out of the shell he'd become, but it wasn't enough, not yet. Look what a simple tree meant to her. He never would have guessed, he never would have known. That's the sort of father he'd become. So hard of a man, he could no longer imagine a child's wonder.

But Felicity could. He bowed his head, his boots heavy in the snow, gripping his cane for balance. He felt weak down to the soul. God may have forgotten him, but He surely watched over Gertie.

I'm grateful to You for that, Lord. More grateful than You know. Surely the Lord was there somewhere. He'd just grown too hopeless to sense Him.

"See, Felicity. See?" Gertie bounced again, bubbling with expectation and turning toward the steps.

He felt her approach before the knell of her shoes on the wet porch steps. She brought the warmth from the house with her and the cheer of the season. She made the lonely places within him ache to be filled.

Shadows fled as she bopped down the stairs with a swirl of her cheerful skirts and the fringe of her shawl swaying.

"Is that what I think it is?" Excitement rang like music in her voice, clear and sweet and true. "You did it. Just like you promised."

"I'm a man of my word. You can always count on that." He'd never thought what it might be like for her to leave everything behind, praying it would be worth the risk. She didn't know what kind of man he would turn out to be. He couldn't explain why it was important to show her who he was, that she had nothing to worry about.

He would always do his best for her. If he had a heart, then she would lay claim to it.

"You found us a wonderful tree, exactly perfect, and it's just the start." Her optimism lilted like lark song. "This Christmas is going to be exceptional. You wait and see, Gertie."

"It's true. It's already happening." Happy tears stood in the child's round eyes. "Last Christmas when the matron drove us all to church, I prayed with all my might. I thought God might hear me the best there, when the choir sang. I promised to be really good, if only next Christmas could be better."

His defenses buckled picturing his daughter without comfort in that church, struggling to believe. He'd been powerless to protect her and regret battered him like a ram. His windpipe closed up, he couldn't speak. All he could do was to lay his free hand on the top of her head, willing what comfort he could into his touch. His poor girl.

"That's all behind you now. The past is gone. It's today that matters." Felicity knew just what to say, and he was grateful for that as she sidled up to the wagon box beside Gertie.

Yes, he was deeply thankful for the lady. When their gazes locked, he read the emotion in her expressive eyes the dark shadows could not hide. Her hand settled on his elbow, a gentle show of caring. Did she know what she did to him? The hard stone of his heart buckled when she smiled.

"How are we going to decorate it?" Gertie asked.

"I have a few ideas, but I'm going to need your help." Felicity peered up at him. "We are going to need a stand of some sort. I'm sure you can come up with something?"

"I'm sure I can." He had free time this evening. Simms hadn't any extra work for him tonight, as business slowed with Christmas's approach. Most folks were turning their thoughts to the holiday and not business. "I need to get Patches rubbed down first."

"After supper, then." Her approval rang in her words, and he couldn't explain why he could sense what she wasn't saying, the appreciation that hovered unspoken in the frigid winter air. He felt it in the squeeze of her hand before she released him, in the slow silence of her smile that turned serious and in the echo in the space where his heart used to be.

"It's a good thing I invited Ingrid and Devin over at the last minute. I had a feeling." She swept away through the falling snow. "We are having a tree-decorating party. Does that sound like fun, Gertie?"

"A real party? Do you mean it, Felicity?" The girl clasped her hands together, overcome. "A real party?"

"Yes, as it's too late for your pa to protest. Here come your aunt and uncle." She offered him a shrug in apology. "Sorry. Maybe I should have given you a warning?"

"No." Choked up, the word twisted on his tongue. He winced, aware of how dark he sounded. It wasn't what he meant. Not by far.

"Aunt Ing! Uncle Devin." Gertie hopped up and down. "We have a tree and a party and everything."

"I told you things would be looking up." Ingrid knelt before the child, careful not to bump her with the sewing basket she carried, and smoothed away a handful of flyaway curls.

The sight of Gertie surrounded by family, circled by love, struck another blow. The girl was flourishing, and his gaze riveted not to his child but to the slender golden-haired woman standing next to her, chatting away with Ingrid. Felicity. He owed her the world. He wished he had as much to give her. He wished he was the man he used to be. For her.

All he could see was her. The way snow caught in her hair and brushed her cheek. The obvious care she felt for Ingrid as they hugged in greeting. The lyrical rhythm of her voice as it sailed on December winds.

"Hey, little brother." Devin trudged around the wagon, heading his way, apparently glad to leave the females to their talking. Hard to miss that know-it-all grin on his face. "On a night like this, seeing Ingrid happy and Gertie laughing again, I can almost believe the hard times might be behind us—that things will start looking up."

"I know the feeling." He grabbed Patches's bridle bits. "My advice is not to get caught up in it. Life is hard. Best to simply accept it."

"Hard times pass, I'm sure they do, and good times come around again."

"I don't know about that."

"You gotta have faith, Tate. Maybe by this time next year, the heartache we've all known will be behind us. That's what I'm praying for." Devin kept pace on the other side of the horse, keeping his voice low so the wind wouldn't carry it back to the women, keeping to the shadows. "Ma and Pa would have adored her."

"Felicity? Yes, and she would have loved them." His throat choked up as it always did thinking about his folks. His mother had passed before the trial and his father after. The strain had been too much. Both of them had died of broken hearts, one right after the other. Unable to say more, he bowed his head. Devin's understanding felt like a lifeline.

He took comfort in the silence that fell between brothers as they broke through the snow on the way to the barn. He felt pulled to Felicity, unable to go the length of the yard without searching for her through the veil of snow.

Her light trill of laughter snared him like a trap. Held captive, unable to blink, he watched as she pretended to race Gertie up the steps and lost, on purpose. Ingrid applauded, while the little girl raised her hands in victory at the top, and yet his attention remained on Felicity.

He was going to let her down. He couldn't stand the thought. He rubbed at the pressure cracking across his chest, thinking over Devin's words. Maybe good times were waiting up ahead. Maybe hardships were behind them, but he feared his marriage to Felicity would be a hardship for her. She wanted love. She deserved love.

He drew Patches to a stop in the lee of the barn, watching as the lamplight spilled across the tiny porch like a carpet of gold at Felicity's feet. She ushered Gertie inside and steered Ingrid in ahead of her. She must have felt the weight of his gaze because she turned, searching for him. Her smile could light up the dark.

She lifted her hand in a fluttery-fingered wave. Love lingered in her wake as she slipped into the house. Her love, not his. His failing, and he hated it. He wanted to love her, he wanted to gaze at her the way she looked at him.

But he had nothing left in him. Nothing of value left to give.

He wished more than anything that he did.

Chapter Nine

"**Y**ou are a wonder, Felicity." Ingrid leaned close to scoop a handful of flatware out of the rinse water. "Look at how happy Gertie is. It's heartening to see."

"She's a doll. I had nothing to do with that. Tate did." She held up a plate to the lamplight, water dripping, and gave it a final scrub. Gertie's happiness heartened everyone and Felicity felt anchored, no longer alone and drifting. She belonged here with these people. After a family supper full of conversation, she was no longer a stranger. She slipped the plate into the rinse water. "Tate raised her. I've done hardly anything at all. Mostly just made a few meals for the girl."

"Oh, you've done a great deal more than that." Ingrid's dark eyes filled with caring. "You have brought her back in a way I couldn't. Don't think I didn't try. She needed you."

"I needed her." That was simply the truth. She might have been lost and forever drifting without that child. Standing at the table she had a good view as Gertie swung open the door, hopping in place, her feet barely touching the floor as she waited for the men to haul in the tree. A mother's affection took deeper root in her heart, an ever-growing love.

"And the difference you've made in Tate…" Ingrid shook her head, tearing up, blinking hard as if fighting strong emotion. "The man released from that prison was not the same one who went in. The man we knew didn't exist anymore. It was as if he'd died, too. Tonight at supper, I saw glimpses of that man again. You have no idea what that means."

"I didn't do so much. I didn't search for his lost daughter. I didn't visit him at the prison. You did that." Felicity set down the dishcloth, remembering their conversation together when she'd first arrived in this house. "You and Gertie would take the train to the prison, so you could see Tate. That's why you were sad."

"Yes. It was hard knowing he was there, knowing he didn't belong behind those bars and leaving him behind. Worse than those things, it was seeing him lose all hope. With every visit, there was less of it. Less of him." Agony lined Ingrid's face, a testimony to the hardship of that time. She shook her head, visibly struggling to erase the emotion. "He's coming back to himself. Look." She nodded toward the door. "He's coming back to us."

"Pa! I've got the door open." Gertie gave another hop. "I've been waiting and waiting for you."

"And letting out all the hot air," Ingrid quipped, chuckling.

Yes, the girl's wide carefree grin and sparkling blue eyes were good to see.

Footsteps knelled on the steps, a cane clunked on the porch. Branches rustled and whispered as the men strong-armed the tree through the doorway, base first. Devin angled in, but it was Tate she saw. No longer a remote mountain of a man, she realized as he ambled out of the shadows. To her, he was larger than life, the center of her world, and everything faded around him, paling until there was only the man shouldering the tree around the door.

I love him so much, she thought. Surely it was happening. He was beginning to love her in return.

"Over here, Pa." Braids bobbing, Gertie bounded across the sitting room. "Put it right there, Uncle Devin."

"You brought Christmas into this house." Ingrid leaned close. "Thank you."

"No, not me. It takes a family to do that, but I'll take credit for the tree. That was my idea." Laughter filled her, a wonderful feeling.

"Is this the right spot?" Devin hunkered down to lower the trunk to the ground, holding it upright. "Right here? I don't want to get this wrong. Tree placement is very important."

"Let me see." Gertie sailed around the tree, bobbing from side to side, the hem of her pink calico skirt springing along with her. "Yep, it's just right. Isn't it, Pa? It couldn't be nicer."

"I agree." Tate bent down on one knee to tweak his daughter's chin. For a moment he looked like someone else, a man she did not know. The granite set to his handsome face softened into a warm and real smile without a trace of sadness. It was easy to see the gentle and loving father he'd been, the one he was now. "Good work, Gertie. Let me get the trunk in the stand I made, and we'll be set to decorate it. Will you do me a favor?"

"Yes. Do you need candles yet? I can get those."

"Great, but not yet." With no shadows to darken him, his eyes shone brighter, not midnight blue but an arresting shade of navy. "First we need to give this tree a drink. Fetch a cup from Felicity and fill it from the water pail."

"Okay!" Determined to do her part, Gertie skipped across the room, too buoyant to simply walk. "Felicity, do you see? Don't you just love the tree?"

"I absolutely do." How she adored this child. The strength of it crashed through her like an ocean, growing ever stronger. She caught the girl's cheek in her hand, love overpowering her at the bliss shining in those wide, dark blue eyes. Tate's eyes.

She felt him across the room like a magnet pulling and her heart responded, turning toward him until he was all she could see. The lamplight glossed his thick dark hair, still in need of a cut, and highlighted the dimples bracketing a smile as he watched his daughter accept a freshly dried cup and saunter over to the water bucket. The unguarded love in his poignant navy-blue eyes riveted her, love for his child.

A reason to adore him more. Gertie dipped the cup, water splashing. What a dear. She couldn't seem to drag her attention away. A brush whispered across her face, not a touch but a sensation. Her pulse tripped, lurching in her chest. Tate watched her. Their gazes connected, freezing time. The room silenced until there was only the beat of shared emotion between them.

There was no affection dazzling in his honest eyes. It was not his love for her that bound them together, but regard did beam from his halting smile. His respect stretched across the room to touch her soul, where it mattered most.

Can you love me? she silently asked.

"This way the tree won't get thirsty." Gertie cradled the full cup in both hands, carrying it with care across the room. "I'm gonna check the water every day, so it stays green and pretty."

"It'll look prettier once you gals get it all decorated." Devin was a less-shadowed version of Tate, quick to grin. "I reckon that means this tree will look dapper before evening's end."

"I'll put the cup down," Tate broke in, accepting the water from his daughter. "If Devin will lift up the tree."

"Sure thing. I might as well make myself useful," his brother quipped.

"Why start now?" Ingrid teased gently. Good-natured laughter rippled through the room as the trio in the sitting area hunkered down to tend to the tree.

The plea remained within her, an innocent long-ing. She dowsed the cloth in the sudsy water and came up with another plate to swipe. Hammer beats of Gertie's shoes reverberated through the room as she skipped around the now-watered tree. Tate watched her, no longer stoic, no longer bleak even in the shadows.

"I'll finish up these last things." Ingrid's suggestion came from very far away, drawing Felicity back.

"What?" She blinked, realizing she still held the plate in mid-rub. "Oh, no. It will only take a few min-utes more with both of us sharing the work."

"Forget it." With affection, Ingrid stole the plate and the cloth. "You go get started with the decorations. Look at that girl. She'll skip herself into exhaustion if you don't."

That wasn't the reason Ingrid sidled into place beside the wash basin.

"Look at Tate." Ingrid's voice fell, too heavy with emotion to carry far. "I'm starting to think love can heal anything. Go to him. Go on."

Tate knelt beside the tree, substantial shoulders wide, one forearm resting on a bended knee, shad-ows gone. Lamplight gravitated toward him, as if to celebrate the moment when the man, who'd been so lost, laughed full and hearty as his daughter twirled like a snowflake whirling around the tree.

"Bravo, Gertie!" Devin called. "Excellent twirling."

"Did you see that, Felicity?" Gertie spun an extra time, the most precious ballerina on earth.

"I saw. Beautiful spin. Are you ready to start decorating?"

"Yes!"

"Then run and fetch the scrap bag from my room."

"Okay. I'll be fast!" The girl took off in a blur of flying braids and jubilation.

"I was worried about decorations." Tate slowly climbed to his feet, leaning on his cane. "I should have known you had something planned."

"Always. I'm full of ideas."

"So I've noticed." A wry touch of humor hooked the corners of his mouth and brought him more to life. The craggy strength of his features and the life force he could not hide softened his hard edges, giving depth to his voice that was no longer hollow.

Breathtaking. He stole more than her breath as he turned away. He had her heart. Tate without his shadows ambled away to talk with his brother, flesh and blood, genuine and real and she could not stop the beat of anticipation that thudded in her ears.

He's coming back to us. Ingrid's thoughts strengthened her as she plucked her sewing basket from the corner. *Please, Lord, let that be true.*

"Here. I got it." Gertie pounded into sight, her arms wrapped around the bulging scrap sack. "Do you have decorations in here?"

"With a little work, we will." Felicity settled on the sofa and opened her sewing basket. "First, look inside to find a red ribbon. It should be right on top."

"Here it is." Gertie held up the thick, cheerful spool of velvet.

"That would make a perfect garland." Ingrid appeared with her sewing basket in the crook of her arm. "It should be long enough to wrap around the entire tree."

"Oh, I want to do it. Can I?" Gertie clutched the thick roll of ribbon hopefully.

"You could, but aren't you a little short for the job?" Devin lumbered over, hooked one arm around the girl's waist and lifted her off the floor. Her squealing giggle made everyone laugh.

"I'm tall enough now," she called as he hefted her high into the air, ribbon trailing. "I'm taller than everyone, even you, Pa. Look."

"I see, shortcake." The nickname tumbled off his tongue, unspoken for so many years. The shock of it rattled him and punched like a fist between his ribs. "You can reach the top of the tree."

"Pa, you called me shortcake." Gertie's hand froze in midair, ribbon dangling, quiet with wonder.

"So I did." The sad girl he'd come home to had faded. He saw it now, the changes that were happening. Even the bitterness began to fade. Maybe he could be the father he'd once been, the father he wanted to be. A smidgeon of tenderness eased up his windpipe and mellowed his baritone. "Why wouldn't I call you shortcake? You're the sweetest girl I know."

"Definitely the sweetest. And a fantastic decorator." Felicity slipped next to him, sweetness, too. Her fingertips rested on his arm, a butterfly touch that made his pulse gallop into a panic. Unaware, she briefly gazed up at Gertie high in Devin's arms, who was busily tucking the ribbon into the tree's high branches. "You're doing a lovely job, Gertie."

"I like it." Gertie adjusted the ribbon a tad, surveying her work. The child was a blur to him. Felicity filled his vision, filled his thoughts, filled his senses. He couldn't focus. Panic raced through his veins. He'd never felt like this before.

"What do you think?" She held up the circle of fabric she'd cut and hung it on a branch. A printed gold snowflake on white fabric dangled by a red thread. "Will it work?"

"It'll do." The words croaked out as if he were choking.

"It looks great from here," Ingrid called, her sewing scissors flashing in the lamplight as she worked. The strain on her round face had faded. For tonight, his sister looked young and carefree, the way a woman her age ought to. For tonight, Devin laughed, the way he used to.

It was Felicity who shone the most. Joy polished her with a rare radiance. She breezed away from him with a flash of a grin and her calico sweetness, talking as she went. Gertie answered with laughter, Ingrid commented and Felicity plopped onto the sofa, creating makeshift beauty out of unwanted scraps.

She was the reason for the laughter in this room, for Gertie's transformation. The hollow where his heart once was throbbed sorely like a broken tooth unable to be soothed. He rubbed his hand over the spot, but the torment did not ease.

Not until her gaze met his. Deep, honest affection glinted in those gentle pools of blue.

Affection he wished he could return. Ashamed, he looked away.

Tate's baritone rumbled pleasantly through the house as Felicity dried the last dessert plate. What a fun time they'd had. She played over the memories, each a treasure to hold dear. Laughing conversations, working alongside Ing making all those decorations, Gertie's glee at the sight of the finished tree, memories she would never forget.

She set the plate on its shelf. The loneliness of her past was gone. She belonged with these people, tonight had proven that. Tonight she'd gained a sister and a brother, to go along with the daughter she already had.

And Tate? Emotionally, he felt a step closer to her. All she wanted was his love.

The mantel clock chimed, breaking into her reverie, reminding her that time was passing. Ingrid and Devin had gone home and the main room echoed with the faint rumble of Tate's baritone. She took a moment to listen, to savor the deep notes and emotion giving his baritone depth. She hung the towel to dry and followed Tate's voice.

Every step she took closer to him made the hook he had in her heart deepen and take better hold. She paused in the doorway, cherishing the sight of him sitting on Gertie's bed. The indomitable breadth of his shoulders, the mighty line of his back and the shaggy length of his dark hair, all so dear to her. Maybe now she could bring up the subject of giving him a trim. After all, that was a task a loving wife did for her husband.

Her husband. The wedding ceremony was merely a technicality, too. Her heart already belonged to him. Tenderness gathered within her so powerfully it blotted out the room, leaving only the glittering brilliance of her feelings. Overwhelmed, she grabbed the doorframe for support.

"One more chapter, Pa. *Please?*"

"Sorry. It's way past your bedtime." The book snapped shut, the tattered volume that had once been Ingrid's favorite book. Gertie had told her so. "Look at you. I see that yawn."

"I can't help it, Pa." One hand covered her mouth. Her face worked, struggling to stifle a yawn. Sleepy eyes were half-shut, but she struggled so hard to stay awake. Nothing on earth could look more endearing than Gertie tucked into bed, with her hair freshly brushed and falling in gold ringlets. Merry was tucked in beside her. "I don't want the day to end."

"I know just how you feel, shortcake."

The little girl took hold of her father's much larger hand. "Was today really real, Pa? Did it happen, or was it just a dream? I'm so happy I can't tell."

"It happened." Tate's voice broke. "You close your eyes and get some sleep. Merry looks tired. She needs her rest."

"Pa?" Gertie held on to him, white-knuckled tight. "We aren't going to lose this house, are we? And have to leave everything behind?"

"No. That's what I'm working hard for. So you can have everything you lost." The shadows clung to him as he leaned down to graze a kiss to his daughter's forehead. "Don't worry. I'm here, now. I won't let anything that bad happen again."

"I know, Pa." The bedclothes rustled as Gertie settled deeper into her pillow, her fingers going slack. "I love you."

"I love you more." Ropes squeaked as he rose from the side of the bed to his impressive height. Towering in the dark, out of the lamp's reach it was hard to see his face. "Sweet dreams."

With a sigh, Gertie snuggled into the covers, already lost in sleep.

She watched his shoulders stiffen, as if he'd finally became aware of her presence in the doorway. He set the book on the night table, his movements slow and deliberate, as if he were biding his time to keep from facing her.

Now that they were alone together, now that he was healing, had his feelings for her changed?

"Felicity." Her name warmed the low notes of his voice. In the dark where it was impossible to read his expression, it was easy to believe he cared. Easy to cling to the fondness gentling his tone. "She was waiting for you to kiss her good-night."

"I'm too late. She's asleep already." Three steps into the room brought her close enough to see the flutter of the girl's long lashes, before her breathing evened out, lost in dreams.

"You should tuck her in tomorrow." Reassuring,

Tate came closer, impossible to see in the inky far reaches of the room, but she could sense his nearness. She turned toward him, drawn by the sound. His cane whispered on the floor. "The coal is stocked up. The water bucket is full for morning."

"Thank you." He was a thoughtful man. He'd taken good care of her from her first night here. She backed into the main room, aware of the child sleeping. "The dishes are done. The kitchen stove's fire is banked."

"Is there anything else I can do for you?"

A thousand things, none of which she could ask him. She wanted to sit in front of the fire with him and talk over the events of the evening, like couples do. She wanted the comfort of his company while she knitted Gertie's mittens. She wanted to know the marvel of his kiss.

"Then you are all set for the night." He sounded more distant, as if the joy of the evening wore off. The shadows closed in, stealing him bit by bit. The man he'd been tonight faded. "I'd best go."

"Wait." She opened a cupboard and pulled out two of her quilts. "The temperature is falling fast outside. I can feel it creep into the room. You may need these tonight."

"I appreciate it." His breathing hitched. He came forward out of the dark, but his face wasn't remote stone. His eyes weren't bleak. He lifted the quilts from her arms. "You bundle up tonight, too."

"I will." Was this how it would always be? Mutual politeness, keeping a safe distance and going their separate ways? She watched him tap away from her, a silhouette outlined by the lamp's glow. He hadn't been like this earlier with his family around.

"I don't know how to thank you for tonight." His boots hesitated halfway to the door. "For what you gave to Gertie."

He didn't turn to face her. In the dark, the indomitable line of his back looked unbreakable, no longer a man of stone but one of steel. Invincible, but not cold.

"I want to give her Christmas." She lifted her chin a notch, grappling for inner strength. "I want her to see that hardships end, that no matter how long or deep the darkness lasts, there isn't a light that can't eventually shine through it."

"You did. You gave that to Gertie. To my family."

Not *our* family. *His* family. She kept her chin up when it wanted to bob down. Maybe he didn't mean that literally, she shouldn't read too much into his choice of words. She wasn't officially a member of this family yet. She stepped into the pool of lamplight, not trusting herself to speak. She had to accept the fact that Tate may be coming back to himself, that he was no longer the man who'd placed an advertisement in the paper. He might be rediscovering his heart and would no longer want a convenient wife.

No longer want her.

"I've got a light day tomorrow. There probably won't be a lot of business at the store." He ambled toward the door, his cane tapping a cautious rhythm. "I'll pick Gertie up from school tomorrow. That will save you a trip."

"All right." She felt as if she were cracking apart. She fought to keep it from showing.

"It's getting late, and you look tired." Another hesitant step.

"I got a lot done today." She was exhausted, but not physically as much as emotionally. He felt further away than ever, more distant than that man on the train platform wanting nothing to do with her.

"So I see. You are a force to be reckoned with."

"I try. You haven't seen anything yet."

"I'm sure." Not icy and not harsh, his tone held a note of warmth, not the cozy kind that a man would use speaking to the woman he was about to marry. But the polite and courteous kind a man uses when speaking with an acquaintance.

The door squeaked open and he merged with the night. He walked away from her easily, when he'd lingered with his brother and sister in their goodbyes and shown such openness at Gertie's bedside, kissing her good-night. For her he didn't look over his shoulder.

"Good night." Not, "I'm looking forward to seeing you in the morning." Not even, "I'm looking forward to another one of your breakfasts." Just the ring of his boots on the porch.

All she wanted was a sign. The smallest encouragement that he might come to care for her, now that his heart was healing. Just something to let her believe this could still work out. That she wasn't about to lose another family, to be torn apart from the man she loved.

Please, Father, just a tiny hint—anything. So I can keep believing.

Nothing. Just a click of the door. Tate was gone, leaving her alone.

The shadows gathered around her, or maybe that was the sorrow's first blow. She eased onto the sofa, determined to do a little knitting on Gertie's mittens, but her hands went to her face instead.

What if Tate was rethinking his decision? He had time to cancel their wedding, it was not Christmas Eve yet. Maybe she had to accept Tate could love again.

He just couldn't love *her.*

She knew you didn't always feel a great loss all at once. It could come in stages, first a great numbing realization. Followed by a crushing strike that booted her between the ribs. Finally came the tearing anguish of her heart shattering. Hope and her dreams leaked out of her.

No, wait, those were tears.

Chapter Ten

He couldn't breathe. Not one squeak of air could slip into his lungs. A colossal invisible anvil had settled on his sternum, allowing nothing in. Nothing out. Every rib he owned felt near to breaking from the unbearable pressure. He eased onto the top step, unable to leave. All he could see was the silvered affection on Felicity's face, her loving regard that he wanted to return.

He sank onto the step, wrapped in failure. The cloying jet-black of the night gave no definition to the world. He leaned his cane against a lower step. Bitter cold radiated up through the wooden planks and nipped on the wind. He felt more like himself. Tonight he'd seen glimpses of the man he used to be.

Glimpses, not the real thing. Not the whole man. But neither was he the bleak shell he'd come to be. Felicity, she was the reason. She lowered his defenses. She softened his hardships. She made him want to believe in fairy tales and the power of love and Christmas miracles. Things he'd given up on. Things he feared he couldn't believe in again.

How did a man summon up something out of nothing? How did he find tenderness in a void? He blew out his breath, frustrated because he didn't know. More than anything, he wished he could believe. He wished he'd stayed inside instead of fleeing out here. He should have responded to the silent plea in Felicity's eyes to stay with her. To sit by the fire, to be the man she needed.

But no, he'd escaped out here where it was easier. Where he didn't have to risk failing her. He ran a fingertip across the scalloped edge of one of her quilts. Soft, pretty, sweet, just like the quilter. A smile touched his lips and softened the dark edges within him. Overhead stars winked out from behind thick clouds, casting a faint silver glow on the yard. On him.

Why don't I feel alone? He rubbed the heel of his hand against his sternum, but the pain remained. *Is that You, Lord? Why can I feel Your presence now?*

The stars twinkled overhead, a heavenly wonder. He tipped his head back to gaze at those white specks strewn against the black. Not a void, after all, but full of blazing light.

Felicity, she'd changed him. No one else could ever have gotten so far inside him. He could feel the difference she made, cracking like thunder behind his ribs. Her radiant smile, her tenacious cheer, her rosebud mouth that looked as soft as satin...

Wait. Where did that thought come from? He placed his hand on his chest, but nothing could ease the torment buried there. The black heartless emptiness remained, a place not even God could touch.

Except that void within him no longer felt black. It was no longer unfeeling. His hopelessness had gone.

What was happening to him? He struggled off the step, teeth chattering, clasping for his cane. The quilts, a light weight in his arm, smelled faintly of roses. Of her. His chest hitched and it was her he saw in his mind's eye, her quiet plea, waiting to be loved.

Impossible hopes ripped him into shreds, that teased him with what could be. That closeness he'd shared with her in the barn the day Gertie played in the snow. That's what could be between them—gentle humor and loving understanding and the tender connection of her soul to his.

That's what he wanted. More than anything. The emptiness was still a part of him as he turned toward the house. Did he go back in? Or did he leave? His grip tightened on his cane. Wanting was not the same as willing. Wanting to love was not the same as having the emotion alive within him. What if his spirit had been too broken? What if he could never fully heal? The windows glowed pink from the ruffled calico curtains, giving him no answer. The wind knifed through him, colder than it had ever been, and his teeth chattered.

He should go home, to his room above the store.

As he turned, he caught a different view of the window. Something he hadn't noticed before. A woman's silhouette fell onto the pink calico, backlit by the lamp. Felicity. Her face was buried in her hands, the perfect picture of devastation, slumped in defeat. Her shoulders shook slightly.

She was crying.

Crying. And he knew why. As the wind knifed him again, he knew the reason why she looked as if she'd lost all hope. Why her unconquerable optimism had failed. She needed a real husband, a man of kindness and heart.

He didn't remember stumbling over the step or crossing the porch. Suddenly the knob was in his hand and the door swung wide. Concern blinded him. Caring cannoned through him, smashing the void within. He could feel it crash like shards of ice and right here, in the center of his chest, welled emotions pure and true.

"Tate." Her blueberry-colored eyes widened. Her rosebud mouth opened in a shocked *O*. Tears tracked down her porcelain cheeks. Embarrassed at being caught, she swiped away the wetness but no amount of blinking stopped those tears.

Those tears broke him. He set down the quilts, his boots ate up the room, all he could see was her. Her misery, her fractured heart. She'd been alone most of her life, weathering hardship and disappointment and dreams that eluded her. She'd loved him when he had no faith in love. She'd given him a home, her kindness and Christmas. The tree held up branches festive with ribbons and bows and snowflakes. And what had he given her?

Not a home, but a house. Not a marriage, but an arrangement. Not her dreams, but the same loneliness she'd always known. But no more. He brimmed over with the wealth of gifts he could give her, freed from the prison of his sorrow. Love for her whispered within him as he went down on his knees before her, a quiet unfolding affection that would not end. It lit the darkest places until he felt basked in light.

"I'm sorry. It's silly of me, a grown woman, crying like this." She swiped at her pearled tears, embarrassment, shame, disgrace stealing the smile from her soft mouth. She sniffled. "Oh, I'm fine. Why did you come back? Do you need something? More blankets, maybe."

"Shh. Don't worry about me. What about you? You don't look all right, darlin'."

"F-fine." Her chin trembled. She fought so hard but her eyes kept welling.

"Then maybe you won't mind if I stay here with you for a while. I could read while you knit. Until it's time for me to head across the street." All he cared about, all he could see, was her. Golden tendrils, blue-tinted agony and the heartbreak wrung across her face. Her beloved face. "Maybe you would like some company?"

"You want to stay? With me?" Furrows dug into her forehead, as if she couldn't figure out why he would ask, a man who did not want her. She blinked back the silvered tears pooled in her eyes, straightened her spine, determined to be strong. "Oh, I understand why you're here. You want to talk."

"I do." He couldn't deny it. Figuring out what to say

and how to say it was tougher to figure out. He had no plan, he was just going on feeling.

"I know it's never going to happen." Vulnerable pain shone through her eyes for a single moment before she shook her head, winning the battle to hide it. "You are never going to be able to love me. I understand."

"I don't think you do."

"It wasn't as if you saw me across a crowded room and fell in love with me. This isn't a fairy tale out of Gertie's book." She shrugged a slender shoulder, a little self-conscious movement, as if to dismiss her hurt, as if to say her risk in coming here was no big deal. "I answered a newspaper advertisement. It was a b-business arrangement. Nothing more."

"I was wrong to say that. I thought it was all I could offer you. I wanted to be honest."

"I know. You are an honest man, Tate." Always caring, even when she was breaking apart. He wasn't going about this the right way.

"I think it's time we amend our business agreement." He took a deep breath. "Render it null and void."

"Of course, as you wish." Her luminous eyes deepened, full of emotion, heavy with sorrow. "I can go on tomorrow's train."

"Go? Why would you want to do that?" Her cheeks were still damp, so he swiped away the remnants of her tears with the pads of his thumbs. Tenderness lived within him with a power that put a burn behind his eyes. "There is something about you that is extraordinary."

"Me, extraordinary? No." She shook her head, gossamer curls catching the light. "There's nothing special about me."

Yes, a man could lose himself in her eyes and never be found again. He wrapped a gossamer tendril around his forefinger and watched it gleam like liquid gold in the lamplight. "*Extraordinary* is too small of a word. I can't think of one single woman in all of existence I would rather be with. I love you, Felicity."

"You love me?" Surprise crumpled her forehead. Agony darkened her eyes, tears she could not let fall, a woman who could no longer believe. His chest hitched in sympathy, his heart alive just like it used to be. He knew a little something about hopelessness.

He cradled her delicate chin in the palm of his hand and lost himself a little more in her gaze. "Even if Gertie hadn't picked you, I would have."

"You would?" The pool of tears rising in her eyes undid him. The faint, rising hope shone through her tears, the heart of the woman, alone all these years, realizing she was loved beyond measure.

"It's the truth. I could never love anyone the way I love you." He leaned in until only a breath separated them, caught in those blueberry-colored depths. "No more marriage of convenience. It's a real marriage I want, a real wedding with love at its center. I want to spend my life showing you exactly how much I treasure you, my beautiful wife."

"Is this real? I'm afraid it's just a dream."

"I think it might be. A dream come true." He leaned in, his lips slanted over hers, his gaze full of love. Love for her.

So gentle, his kiss. His lips brushed hers like a blessing, faithful and true. Reverence filled her, a strong abiding affection that brimmed her heart and soothed her soul. She let her hands fall to his chest and beneath the bulk of his coat she knew his heart beat only for her. She let herself believe.

When he lifted his lips from hers, neither of them moved. The fire roared in the stove, the shadows faded from the room until there was only the two of them and the love soft on his face.

Love. She'd never seen anything as strong or true.

"I have a question to ask. It's an important one." His gaze held hers, full of sparkling emotion. The desolation was gone. Only grand affection blazed where despair had once lived. His smile gentled the sculpted handsomeness of his face, that was no longer stone. "Will you be my bride? Gertie and I can't be a family without you."

"Yes. I love you, Tate. I will always love you." Dazzling joy sparkled through her, chasing away every sadness and leaving only hope. Not all loves lasted, but this one would. She could feel it in the poignant sweetness when he leaned closer to kiss her again. The lamplight flared, as if in a blessing, and she remembered to thank God for Tate's love, the best Christmas gift ever.

Epilogue

Christmas Eve

Tate Winters tipped the brim of his Stetson to get a better look at the vestibule door. He couldn't wait for his bride to come down that aisle. The church echoed around him with anticipation, and the flicker of candlelight fell like grace, a grace he could feel. He braced his shoulders, preparing for the best.

A commotion rose up in the vestibule, out of his sight, but the faint rush of the outside wind announced Felicity's presence. A door whispered shut and light footfalls padded closer. With his heart whole, he turned toward the doorway, at peace. For a while there, hopelessness had gotten the best of him, but no more. Never again.

"Pa, do you see her?" Gertie clutched his hand, her fingers small and slight within his own. "That's my new ma."

"Yes, she is." His precious bride. Pure happiness

filled him, the greatest he'd ever known. He drank in the sight of the cheerful woman in a light blue dress breezing his way. Slender, graceful, lovely. Perfection. Nothing on earth had ever been so beautiful.

Hard to believe such a lady would marry him. But he knew exactly how he'd gotten so lucky—God had been watching over him and Gertie all along. He just hadn't been able to feel it. He could now. He no longer felt alone as he watched Felicity hurry down the aisle toward them.

"She's like a princess." Gertie looked captivated, blue eyes wide, button face hopeful, new dress swishing as she turned. "This is just like one of the stories in my books, Pa."

"It surely is." He knew what it was like, that tingly feeling of realizing what you were about to get in life was far greater than anything you could imagine. He was grateful his daughter was about to get her dream.

And so was he.

"Sorry to keep you waiting. Ingrid wouldn't stop fussing but she assures me it was worth it. Whew. I couldn't make the horse get here fast enough." Felicity's melodious alto lifted into the air, sweet as church music. "I feel as if I've been waiting for the two of you all my life."

"All my life," he agreed. Captivated, he could not look away. Snowflakes clung to her golden hair, fairytale diamonds for the storybook princess. He could see their future stretching out before him. A happy marriage, more children, a life lived full and loving and well. He intended to spend the rest of his days cherishing his wife. She was his heart, his soul, his everything. He would be nothing if she had not stepped off that train.

"Aunt Ingrid, do you see my new dress?" Gertie gave a little swirl to show off the creation of ruffles and lace.

"I see. It's lovely. The best dress ever." Ingrid slipped into the front pew next to Devin. Both beamed with happiness and approval.

The groom held out his hand to take the bride's. Anyone observing would be touched by the powerful and poignant looks of affection they gave to each other. It was a blessed moment as the bride swished to face the pulpit. The church silenced, souls stilled and heaven waited.

"Are you two ready?" Reverend Hadly asked kindly.

"More than ready." As if she were floating, her feet didn't seem to touch the floor. Joy sweetened the moment when Tate turned toward her, his eyes fastening on hers. Endless love sparkled between them. "I've waited most of my life for this moment. For this gift."

"Me, too." Tate smiled gently, as if he also saw their future. Laughter in the snow, tender moments, Christmases gathered around the tree, and as the years passed one thing would remain. Their love.

"Then let's begin." Reverend Hadly opened his Bible.

"Wait! Wait! There's one more thing." Braids bobbing, Gertie rushed up and held out both hands, one for her father and one for her mother.

For me, Felicity thought. Bliss touched her like grace. She was grateful to God for this one perfect moment when the candles seemed to burn more brightly as if to bless their union. That brightness surrounded them with an incandescent glow.

"Merry Christmas, my bride," Tate whispered.

"Merry Christmas." Wherever life took them, she knew their love would see them through. Nothing was stronger than the abiding affection binding them, soul to soul.

"Dearly beloved," the reverend began, making them husband and wife, making them a family.

Forever.

* * * * *

Dear Reader,

Welcome back to Angel Falls. When Janet Tronstad and I teamed up with the idea to write an anthology together, I had no idea how much fun it would be, or the places in the heart where this novella would take me. *Her Christmas Family* is about loss and love, about love's power to heal even the most broken hearts. It's a story about a little girl wanting a mother for Christmas and getting a family. I've had this story in my heart for years, and I'm grateful for the chance to finally write it. I hope you enjoy this Christmas tale where God's love shines bright.

Thank you for choosing *Her Christmas Family*.

Wishing you peace, joy and love this holiday season,

Jillian Hart

Questions for Discussion

1. What was your first impression of Tate? How would you describe him? What do you like most about his character?

2. How would you describe Felicity and Tate's first meeting? What did you learn about Felicity's character? What did you learn about Tate's?

3. Why is Felicity the right ma for Gertie?

4. What does Tate fear most?

5. What is the story's predominant imagery? How does it contribute to the meaning of the story? Of the romance?

6. Do you see God at work in this story? Where and how, and what meaning do you find there?

7. How would you describe Tate's faith? Does it change throughout the course of the book? How would you describe Felicity's faith?

8. What do you think Tate and Felicity have each learned about love?

CHRISTMAS STARS
FOR DRY CREEK

Janet Tronstad

This book is dedicated to my new Twitter and Facebook friends. Who knew it would be so much fun? Look me up if you haven't already.

Now after Jesus was born in Bethlehem of Judea in the days of Herod the king, behold, wise men from the east came to Jerusalem, saying, Where is he who has been born king of the Jews? For we saw his star when it rose and have come to worship him.
—*Matthew* 2:1–2

Chapter One

Montana Territory, December 1884

Winter sun filtered into the old cabin, bringing a faint light to Eleanor McBride as she sat by the empty fireplace and frowned. Her fingers were stiff from the cold, but that wasn't the problem. She had been knitting a star with yarn she'd brought with her to this remote place and, no matter how much she twisted the yellow threads, it wasn't going to hang properly on the pine tree she had dragged inside just yesterday. Other women might know how to make a star, but she didn't. She finally laid her knitting needles down in her lap and acknowledged the bitter truth.

She was a failure at making Christmas.

Of course, she had done everything she could, she told herself as she looked around the poorly furnished dwelling. The man who had sent for her to be his wife would just have to be satisfied with that. After all, there was no holly to make a wreath for the rough-hewn door and no lime to whitewash the cracked walls to show respect for any travelers who might visit them here. However, she had managed the most important thing: she had saved her last candle so they'd have a light to place in the window on the holy night.

She always felt as if God counted his children by looking at those candles.

She wondered briefly if the man, Sergeant Adam Martin, cared about candles or stars or even the Holy Child himself. She had not met him yet and knew so little about him, only what he'd written in that one rather awkward letter. He'd said then that he wanted her to get his house ready for Christmas, but it was more because of his seven-year-old daughter, Hannah, than himself.

A calico kitten meowed at Eleanor's feet and she bent to pick it up. Its soft fur was the same copper color as her wild Irish hair. The promise of the daughter had been what made her leave a quiet life on the Stout estate and come west to marry a stranger who lived in this house near Dry Creek.

A glance up at the only window in the room showed her that the sky had been growing steadily darker as she sat there until now its gray expanse put her in mind of the sheep storms they used to have back home in Nantucket. The fog was so thick and heavy during those times that it drenched the thick coats of the animals. She sorely missed the island. Even the air here seemed different; it was more brittle somehow, and this morning she had felt the pinch of it in her breath as she walked down to the creek.

She hoped she'd be happy in this place. She was thirty-five years old and this might be her last chance to be a mother and have a family. After her father died several months ago, she had been keenly aware in her grief that she had no one left who belonged to her. She had never given much thought to getting married when he'd been alive.

Not that she'd had many chances to wed. Even when she'd been younger, men had been reluctant to court her. Her red hair was not fashionable enough for most people. She refused to wear a corset or hide her face from the sun even though she freckled. Those men who weren't put off by that seemed to back down when they saw how direct her green eyes were. They said she saw too much, and it made them nervous.

Of course, the sergeant had never seen her eyes.

"I'm beginning to think something is wrong, though," she murmured as she stroked the cat's soft fur. "That man should be here by now."

According to the letter, the sergeant's daughter had been staying with his mother in Ohio and was supposed to be coming home this Christmas to finally live with him. But Eleanor had been waiting for twelve days and no one, not the sergeant nor his child, had stepped through the cabin's door. The neighbors who had met her at the train station said he was out on one last patrol with his troops before his replacement got here. But she was no longer convinced that explained his absence.

"Maybe he changed his mind about marrying a

woman he doesn't know," she said to the kitten in her lap as it closed its eyes and began to purr.

She didn't completely blame the sergeant. After all the time she had spent coming out here on the train, she still wasn't sure about the arrangement herself. So much was unknown. His daughter might not be as wonderful as the man said in his letter. He hadn't mentioned the land, but it was more flat and barren than she had imagined. Even when frozen, she could tell by the way the dry soil crumbled between her fingers that it wouldn't be fertile enough to grow much besides scrub grass come spring.

Just then Eleanor heard the sound of a wagon outside. She set the kitten down on the floor before stepping over to the fireplace and picking up the poker. It was the only weapon she had unless she counted her knitting needles. Or the rifle in the back room. She forced herself to take a deep breath. She would get the gun if needed, but she had little experience with it.

The footsteps on the porch gave her pause. A neighbor would knock at the door, but she heard the sounds of a rattle. Someone was testing the latch. She kept the latch drawn when she was inside even though she had to leave the door unsecured when she left for any reason. Not that there was anything worth stealing inside the cabin. A crude table. A rope-tied bed in the back room with some furs and army blankets draped over it. A cast-iron cook stove that didn't heat properly, and the stool she'd been sitting on. And, of course, her father's old telescope that he'd given her before he died. It was carefully wrapped in a length of her best black flannel and tucked in her valise, waiting for the next clear night.

The door rattled again, this time more impatiently. She would not give up the telescope without a fight. That, along with her mother's old opera gloves, was all she had of her family. Maybe she should get the rifle, after all.

"Let me in," a man's voice demanded.

She relaxed some. If she'd ever heard a military voice, this was it. But she couldn't be too careful. "Who is it?"

"Sergeant Adam Martin, ma'am."

She could almost hear the click of his boots, but she still hesitated. Since she'd never met him, she had no idea what his voice should sound like.

"Could you say that again?" she asked to give herself more time to think. She wished she could ask him a question that would prove he was who he said. It was a little unnerving to realize she knew nothing about him that everyone else within miles of here didn't already know. Except for one thing.

"What's my name?" she demanded to know.

There was silence on the other side of the door for a moment, but he finally answered, "Eleanor Hamilton."

"McBride," she corrected him, wondering how he knew her mother's maiden name. The Hamilton family surely didn't claim her any more than they had her mother.

"Just let me in." The man's voice was impatient.

A woman's voice rose in the distance then, too. "What's wrong, dear?"

Eleanor's heart sank. Maybe it wasn't the gamble of it all that had stopped him. Maybe the sergeant had found someone else to marry. Someone younger. Prettier. More biddable. Although a man desperate enough to advertise for a wife should have already exhausted his circle of acquaintances before placing his advertisement, she thought in exasperation. She knew such a man was likely to have any number of problems, but she had never thought he might be slow-witted.

Eleanor stepped toward the door, and then stopped to place the fireplace poker against the wall before unlatching the door and opening it. She didn't want him to know she'd been afraid.

"Oh." She blinked.

It had been snowing and a light dusting of white covered the dark military coat he wore. He had a scowl on his face, but his black hair showed thick as he held his cap in his hands and his blue eyes were so handsome that she felt a little faint. He was not at all like she expected.

"You're the man who wrote the letter?" she asked, and then cleared her throat to take the wispy quality away. This man should have had no trouble finding a spouse even in a place like this. If he had gone back East, the young women would have lined up to marry him.

She took another look at him and frowned. What had her late employer, Mrs. Stout, been thinking? The other woman had been the one to answer the ser-

Dear Reader,

We hope you've enjoyed reading
this inspirational historical
romance novel. If you would like
to receive more of these great
stories delivered directly to your
door, we're offering to send you
two more of the books you love so
much, **plus** two exciting Mystery
Gifts – absolutely **FREE!**

Please enjoy them with our
compliments...

Jean Gordon

Editor,
Love Inspired Historical

**Peel off seal and
place inside...**

HOW TO VALIDATE YOUR
EDITOR'S FREE GIFTS!
"THANK YOU"

1 Peel off the FREE GIFTS SEAL from the front cover. Place it in the space provided at right. This automatically entitles you to receive two free books and two exciting surprise gifts.

2 Send back this card and you'll get 2 Love Inspired® Historical books. These books are worth $11.50 in the U.S. or $13.50 in Canada, but are yours absolutely FREE!

3 There's no catch. You're under no obligation to buy anything. We charge nothing—ZERO—for your first shipment. And you don't have to make any minimum number of purchases—not even one!

4 We call this line Love Inspired Historical because every month you'll receive books that are filled with inspirational historical romance. This series is filled with engaging stories of romance, adventure and faith set in historical periods from biblical times to World War II. You'll like the convenience of getting them delivered to your home well before they are in stores. And you'll love our discount prices, too!

5 We hope that after receiving your free books you'll want to remain a subscriber. But the choice is yours—to continue or cancel, anytime at all! So why not take us up on our invitation, with no risk of any kind. You'll be glad you did!

6 And remember...just for validating your Editor's Free Gifts Offer, we'll send you 2 books and 2 gifts, *ABSOLUTELY FREE!*

YOURS FREE!
We'll send you two fabulous surprise gifts (worth about $10) absolutely FREE, simply for accepting our no-risk offer!

The Editor's "Thank You" Free Gifts Include:

- Two inspirational historical romance books
- Two exciting surprise gifts

YES!

PLACE FREE GIFTS SEAL HERE

I have placed my Editor's "thank you" Free Gifts seal in the space provided above. Please send me the 2 FREE books and 2 FREE gifts for which I qualify. I understand that I am under no obligation to purchase anything further, as explained on the opposite page.

102/302 IDL FH7E

Please Print

FIRST NAME

LAST NAME

ADDRESS

APT.#

CITY

STATE/PROV.

ZIP/POSTAL CODE

The Reader Service—Here's How It Works:

geant's advertisement, not telling Eleanor about it until the man had sent his letter proposing marriage. Even at that, she had been prepared to accept a misfit. She was one herself, after all.

But a man like this and her? His coat might be a little rough from travel, but he looked every inch an Eastern gentleman with his shoulders squared and his hands in leather gloves that must have cost considerably more than any shoes she'd ever had on her feet.

The Stout estate had been a humble place and she wasn't used to men like him. Frankly, she'd have preferred a husband who slouched. Or a working man like her father with clothes in need of mending and windblown hair that needed trimming. She'd be able to work at redeeming such a man. She didn't have anything to offer the one who stood in front of her.

"Of course it's me," he snapped as if he thought she was the one who was dimwitted.

Strangely enough, that made her feel better. Maybe it was his bad temper that accounted for his trouble in finding a wife.

"Well, are you going to let us in or not?" he demanded.

Eleanor smiled and stepped aside. "Please, do come in."

Yes, she thought to herself, his disposition was clearly the problem.

Sergeant Adam Martin was cold, hungry and in no condition to face the realization that he had promised to marry a lunatic. He'd taken his mother's word that

Eleanor whatever-her-last-name-was would be, above all, a competent woman who could be trusted with the gentle sensitivities of an invalid child. Right now, he wasn't so sure he could trust her to stable his horses. She was acting as if she hadn't expected him to be here, and this was his house.

He stomped the snow off his boots and walked inside. He'd bought the place and all its contents in early fall from an old man who'd decided to move back to the mountains even if the trapping wasn't what it used to be. The weather had been fine then, and the sergeant hadn't realized how much work would be necessary for anyone to live here comfortably in a harsh winter. Even if he had, there had been no time to make any repairs while he was finishing his duties with the army.

Looking at the cabin now, though, he saw that it wasn't much better than the shelter that had been added to the back side of the house for the sake of the animals. Something needed to be done and soon. The walls were made of unpeeled logs that had grown gray and drafty over the years. On the outside, prairie sod was piled around the bottom half of the building, but inside the cracks on the upper half were filled with little more than dried clay. Railroad spikes had been driven into the corners to keep the logs steady. The chimney, though not mortared, was all that seemed sturdy enough to survive the winter.

"Why don't you have a fire going?" he asked when he took his gloves off and suddenly realized the air inside was just as cold as it had been out on the porch.

Maybe it was even colder since the porch at least had the benefit of what sun had been there earlier in the day.

"I didn't want the needles on the Christmas tree to get brown," the woman explained as though it should be obvious. She eyed his hands, and he wondered if he was supposed to ask permission before he bared his hands in her presence. His late wife had been adamant about such things. They might live in the West, she'd say, but that was no excuse for them to forget the rules of polite society. She had been determined to raise Hannah to be a proper lady and he had sworn to do everything he could to honor that wish in her absence.

Only then did the sergeant see the spindly pine tree standing in one corner of the cabin in the bucket he had planned to use if he was able to buy a cow for milking. The tree had some odd-shaped pieces of yellow yarn strewn about on its branches.

Just then a kitten ducked out from behind the woman's skirts and ran, as best it could while dragging one of its legs, until it could hide behind the bucket.

"What was that?" he asked in bewilderment.

"That's our—my, I mean—my cat," the woman said defiantly, and then added, "I found him at the railroad station where you were supposed to meet me. His leg was hurt in an accident, and it's too cold to put him outside now."

She stepped between him and the kitten as though

the bucket wasn't enough to stop him from hurting the little thing.

"It's too cold inside, too," the sergeant said, deciding to ignore the unfounded accusation. He'd never deliberately hurt an animal in his life. He'd worked with enough raw recruits, though, to recognize the expression on the woman's face. She wasn't going to take orders from him even though she knew she would be court-martialed if she refused. Well, he supposed, no one really court-martialed wives who didn't obey, but it was the same philosophy. In battle, men all needed to obey one commander or everyone died. He figured it wasn't that much different in civilian life.

He felt a headache coming on. Maybe the woman didn't realize all that was happening. "My mother's outside. And my daughter. Is there dry wood for a fire?"

He'd learned to keep things simple for the new recruits.

The woman's face lit up. "Hannah is here?"

He nodded, and the tension in his head receded. This woman, Eleanor, might be slow in some respects, but pure love shone out of her eyes when she asked about his daughter. His little girl needed that kind of softness almost as much as she required someone to guide her into womanhood.

Before he could say more, Eleanor ran out the door toward the wagon he'd parked outside. The two horses stood patiently in the snow. He had hoped to introduce his mother more carefully to his bride. Even though his mother had been the one to choose from the several letters he'd received in response to his advertisement, she was seldom satisfied with anything. So he figured he better get out there and do what he could to protect his bride-to-be.

"Whatever happened to you?"

The sergeant could hear his mother's booming voice from the doorway. It started with dismay and was moving into disbelief by the time he got to the wagon. His mother was eyeing Eleanor with horror.

The gray clouds had parted and the sun was shining through but neither woman seemed to notice that the day had warmed. One of the horses lifted its head as the sergeant grew near.

"You can't be Eleanor." His mother ended her pronouncement and turned her glare in his direction. "Look at her hair. No lady would ever go about with her hair loose like that. She's an impostor. Don't let her near Hannah."

At the mention of her name, his daughter shuddered and seemed to shrink deeper into the buffalo robe he'd brought to keep them warm on the ride home from Miles City. His mother had that effect upon children, which was the main reason he was anxious to have his daughter with him. She might be scarred from the fire, but it pained him more to see her becoming so timid.

"How could Eleanor be an impostor?" The sergeant tried to keep his voice mild as he turned back to the women. He hadn't taken in the sight of her hair until now and the vision of it caught him unprepared. It was magnificent, shining like pure copper in the sunlight.

He felt his lips warm into a smile. Green eyes and ample hips completed the picture.

Then he suddenly realized she must be freezing. The gray flannel dress she wore couldn't be warm enough, especially without a cloak. The ladies he knew complained of a slight breeze. But this woman didn't seem aware of the temperature.

"I don't know how she did it," his mother declared, pointing at Eleanor before turning to him. "Maybe she changed places with someone on the train. I've heard of that. People get to talking and telling each other their life stories and one of them sees a chance to improve their lot by doing away with the other. Things happen on trains."

Eleanor gasped at that.

"Are you accusing me of murder?" she demanded, taking a step closer to the wagon. "I met a very nice young woman on the train, Felicity Sawyer. And I can guarantee she is still very much alive in Angel Falls, Montana. I'm expecting a letter from her any day."

"Now, Mother," the sergeant added as he tore his gaze away from the woman. "You were the one who corresponded with Mrs. Stout and found out about Eleanor. She's who she's always been."

"No, she's not. She's supposed to be a Hamilton," his mother practically wailed. "Mrs. Stout said she was the granddaughter of the real Hamiltons. The ones in Boston. The ones who matter."

The sergeant could see Eleanor grow pale before his eyes. With her mass of red hair, her translucent skin was really quite distracting. He thought it was the cold that had made her blanch until he saw the twitch in her jaw.

When she spoke her voice came out deep and indignant. "My mother was the one who mattered. Those Hamiltons, her parents, had nothing to do with her after she married my father. They didn't want an Irish gardener in their family no matter how learned he was. He was good enough to tend their roses, but not to court their daughter. He was a brilliant man and my mother's parents were nothing but pompous, idiotic fools. Not that they'd have asked my opinion on it—or anything else in this world."

His mother just sat there in the wagon, her deep gray cloak wrapped close around her neck and her mouth hanging open in protest. At first, he thought the shock she seemed to be feeling was because she wasn't used to anyone talking back to her and he could see Eleanor wasn't retreating an inch. He found that admirable in a recruit, even if it was a little dangerous when they did so before assessing the battlefield.

His mother finally closed her mouth, only to open it again a moment later. "You mean the Hamiltons don't talk to you at all? *Ever?*"

Eleanor shook her head. "Not one word since I was born. I do hear they talk *about* me, though. No one would hire my father or me because of it on the mainland. Mrs. Stout was the only one brave enough to risk their scorn. Out on Nantucket Island, the Hamilton family didn't matter so much as it did in Boston."

His mother pressed her lips together in a tight line. "I'm not concerned about the Hamiltons," the sergeant said, feeling he needed to step in before his mother dismissed the woman over something that was not important. Even his late wife wouldn't be particular about society gossip concerning something that happened so long ago. "After all, I'm assuming you were born after they split from her family and your parents were rightfully married."

The woman turned her affronted gaze upon him. "I assure you that I have papers in my valise to prove both their wedding and my birth date. They are respectable. My father was an honorable man. I'll not have anyone say otherwise."

He put up his hand in surrender. He wasn't quite sure why he'd even asked, except for the fact that an irregular birth might make it difficult for the woman to chaperone Hannah at the kind of balls and parties she'd need to attend when she was grown. All of which were years away.

His mother seemed to recover a little. "Well, I suppose we need to make the best of things now that you're here. And you do have your time with Mrs. Stout. She never said what your position was. I suppose it was as a governess, though. Or maybe a companion."

Eleanor shook her head and lifted her chin higher. "I assisted my father with tending the sheep after my mother died. I was younger than Hannah there when I first went to the fields." She nodded toward his daughter and then defiantly turned back to his mother. "My father and I were perfectly happy for all those years until he got a fever and died. Mrs. Stout kept me on while I tried to find something else, but her husband's nephew is taking over the estate soon, and he won't stand for a female shepherd so she thought I might like the West. I've nothing to be ashamed of, though. Quite the opposite. I can shear a wild ram all by myself if need be. I can cord the wool. Dye it. Then weave it into some of the softest flannel you'll ever see."

There was absolute silence after the woman finished her speech. The sergeant feared his mother's face looked a little purple, but it was hard to tell because the feathers on her hat kept bobbing in front of her. He had to admit, though, that he was having his own doubts about how suitable Eleanor was going to be.

Finally, a little voice spoke up from the middle of the buffalo robe. "Did you have a lamb?"

Hannah never talked to strangers, and the sergeant was glad to see Eleanor didn't rush over and frighten his daughter. Instead, she smiled very nicely and nodded. "Yes, I had a beautiful black lamb and some white lambs, too. I miss them."

Hannah sighed and ducked back inside the robe.

The sergeant felt like sighing, too. For the first time since he'd collected his mother and daughter from the train station, he had hope that Hannah would learn to live again. If she could talk to a stranger, she could get better. Maybe the woman could help, after all.

"Surely you can't expect to marry my son," his mother said, turning again to glare at Eleanor. "I wouldn't feel comfortable leaving Hannah in the care of someone who worked with—with animals. I mean if you were riding horses in the park—that would be one thing. But sheep? Goodness. You won't be able to teach her anything. No needlepoint. No music. No manners."

The sergeant suddenly realized how offensive his mother sounded. The woman might not be what he'd expected, but he didn't want her to leave. He'd caught the wistful look in Hannah's eyes before she buried her face in the robe.

"Speaking of manners," he said stiffly as he turned toward Eleanor. "I'd like you to meet my mother, Mrs. Abigail Martin. She'll be returning to her home in Ohio a week or two after Christmas."

Then he turned to the woman who'd given him birth. "Mother, I'd like you to meet my future wife, Eleanor Hamilton."

"McBride," the woman spoke up, looking none too happy with him.

He'd forgotten how prickly women could be. So he added, "I should say that I hope she'll be my wife."

Then he turned the smile on her that he'd given women back in his courting days. It had been a long time since he'd tried to be gallant, but back then they'd said his smile melted hearts up and down the county. He'd never had reason to doubt it until now.

His future wife glared at him. "I don't know how to knit much, either."

And, with that, she turned and stomped back to the cabin, her dress swaying enough to make him grin. She had some fire to her, this woman who'd said she'd marry him.

His mother grunted in disgust when she saw his face. He didn't pay her any mind, though. He was focused on Eleanor. He was hoping she wouldn't, but she did slam the door after she marched inside. He didn't relish going back up there and knocking, but he had little choice.

So he put his hat back on his head. A good soldier always did his duty whether he wanted to or not. He started walking toward the door. She'd probably latched it again, too. He wondered if she'd open it any quicker if he called her sweetheart when he knocked. He grinned, just thinking about it. A good military man always had a strategy or two up his sleeve.

Chapter Two

Eleanor wasn't responsible for the bare shelves in what served as a cupboard and she hoped that man realized it. There was no flour, sugar, coffee, tea or anything else a lady like his mother would consider worthy of eating. Some dried herbs were still packed away in Eleanor's valise and she had found some potatoes and carrots in the shelter behind the house. They were withered, but edible if a person wasn't too fussy.

A few days ago, after she'd brushed aside some snow down by the creek, she had found wild onions. She'd even caught a few trout when she first arrived. Of course, the weather had grown colder and she hadn't tried to fish since then. She'd had to break ice on the creek this morning just to get water.

"There's still some of the bacon your neighbors brought over to me," Eleanor said, knowing she should try to be more agreeable. She'd been teased often enough in her life; she shouldn't have let that "sweetheart" of his bring a blush to her cheeks. She looked up at him and added. "Sir."

He seemed startled by that. "You can call me Adam."

She nodded, satisfied that she could unsettle him, too.

"I have beans simmering on the stove." His mother and daughter were in the back room and she wanted to let him know what she had. She kept her voice quiet, in case he didn't want them to know how scarce their food was. "I'll add a bit of the bacon for tonight."

"Beans?" he frowned and lowered his voice, too. "I sent an order for supplies to the mercantile before I left on patrol."

"Nothing has come while I've been here." The knowledge that he had given more than a passing thought to her arrival softened her mind toward him somewhat, though. "Maybe it's still coming."

"I doubt it. They could have hauled the supplies out here on foot in the amount of time they've had. The message must not have gotten to them. The old man who sold me this place said he'd leave some cans of peaches when it came time for him to head out."

"He did that." Eleanor had found the bag of pinto beans, too, in the shelter behind the cabin. She'd thought they had been overlooked by whoever had lived here before, but now she realized they'd been left as a kindness, as well.

The sergeant opened the firebox of the old stove and put a handful of twigs inside before shutting it again.

"And you need more wood, too. Didn't the Hargroves stop by and see how you were doing?"

Eleanor nodded. "A couple of times."

"Well, knowing them, they must have asked if you had everything you needed."

"They did. I told them I was fine. The bacon was a present, they said. That's why I accepted it."

He grunted at that, but didn't say any more.

She was glad to see his gaze had returned to the nearly empty wood box. She'd only used a small fire when cooking because she feared running out of fuel to burn. There was a grove of trees down in the gully to the left of them by the creek, but she hadn't been strong enough to pull any of the fallen trees back to the cabin. The sergeant could use the wagon and horses to do that. She wanted to see how the stove took to a full fire before she tried to bake anything like biscuits in it. The furniture and other things in the cabin had all been used to the point of breaking so she didn't have much confidence in the stove, especially since it seemed to heat unevenly.

"Well, it's beans for supper, then, I guess," he said softly as he finally looked up at her.

She was silent for a moment. His face was tense and she didn't know why. Maybe he was embarrassed to have nothing else to serve his mother. She bristled with the thought that he would blame her for that until she remembered how prickly her father had been when he'd made a mistake. He'd be the same way if his supplies hadn't come through.

"Don't worry," she said. "Christmas won't be here for two more days."

"I'm sorry," he replied. "I should have taken the message to the mercantile myself. I'll make a trip to Miles City tomorrow to buy what we need."

Eleanor nodded. She felt better getting to know his ways. "I gave some of the peaches to the Hargroves when they brought me the bacon. Maybe I shouldn't have."

"I'm glad you did," he said, some of the tension leaving him, as well.

"They're good neighbors," he added and smiled at her as if she was somehow responsible for that.

Eleanor stopped in mid-fret. She might trust him a little more since he had some of the same failings as her father, but she didn't want him to feel as if he had to pretend they were a normal engaged couple. She was going to be mothering his daughter; she expected to love Hannah. But she hadn't decided how she would feel about him yet. It was easiest to see him as her new employer. Either way, he didn't need to smile so much and she ought to tell him that.

"I can make a peach cobbler," she heard herself say instead, and then, lest he read too much into that, she added, "We need something special for Christmas. Or, if you'd rather, I could make a plum pudding if you get the ingredients."

Because of her father's Irish pride, English puddings had been strictly forbidden when she prepared meals in the sheepherder's wagon. On the holiday, she'd serve up a nice spiced beef brisket roasted over the fire and they'd talk of the Christmas cake he remembered from his childhood. But the cook in the Stout kitchen had said she'd known plenty of Irish who enjoyed an English pudding and she'd shown Eleanor how to make one when the staff had found out she was going West. She'd also shown her how to roast a Christmas goose and make a hard sugar candy. Not that Eleanor was likely to find a goose wandering around this country, but when she got some sugar she might attempt the candy. Mrs. Stout had given her a small bottle of peppermint oil to use in it if she got the chance.

Just then Adam's mother swept aside the curtain that separated the main part of the house from the back room that held the bed. "I've always thought a Christmas called for meringue."

"We don't have any eggs, Mother," Adam said.

"Well, surely for Christmas—" She turned and looked at Eleanor. Some of the purple had gone out of the woman's face and she looked genuinely concerned. "Hannah expects a proper Christmas dinner. I always make a sour cream raisin pie with meringue. It's her favorite."

"She'll find a new favorite," Adam said in a tight voice. "This is the West. Things are different."

"Not so different that you can ignore a little girl's Christmas," his mother said as she turned around. "I just hope Hannah is sleeping and doesn't hear any of this."

Having made her disapproval clear, his mother marched into the back room.

There was a moment of silence after that.

"I'm sorry, I—" Adam ran his fingers through his hair as he kept looking at the curtain. "My mother will be out here again once she's made sure Hannah is down for her nap." He looked at Eleanor. "I'm afraid she'll be here through Christmas, but we'll be fine. Get a good night's sleep and—" he stopped and paused a moment and looked around "—I'm sorry. I guess I need more beds. I had planned to fetch Hannah myself, but my mother decided to bring her here so she could—ah—meet you."

Eleanor lifted her chin. This all was hardly her fault. "Even with just Hannah here, we would need more beds. You have only the one stool, too."

She should have realized what it meant to see that sole stool standing alone in the middle of the floor when she first entered this place. Adam might have written her the letter asking her to marry him and he might have sent her the money to buy a railroad ticket out here, but he hadn't given any thought at all to what their life together would be like. Even Mrs. Stout had given more consideration to this new life; in addition to the peppermint oil she'd placed in her valise, the older woman had given her a dozen linen handkerchiefs and a book on raising a lady so Eleanor would know what to do for her young charge.

She watched Adam look around the room as though he hadn't noticed until now that it was furnished for one lonely old man who never even had company for dinner.

"Those trunks I put in the back room—the ones

that have Hannah's things. We can sit on them," he finally said.

"I have some lengths of flannel that I can drape over them," Eleanor said, offering what she could. As an early Christmas gift, Mrs. Stout had given her back some of the cloth she had woven this fall. "They're nothing fancy, but most of them are a nice sheep's gray. And warm. I could add some red ribbon to the corners to make them festive. And they'll keep everyone's clothes clean and prevent any snags from the trunks."

"Good," he said quietly, but she could see that his heart wasn't in it. He looked tired. "The ribbon will be nice. A woman's touch is what we need to make this a home."

"The ribbon is a little worn," she added, determined to be truthful.

What had she done? Eleanor wondered. She'd never thought the man she was setting out to marry would worry about ribbons. She'd grown up in a sheepherder's wagon; she never felt she quite belonged in houses that had what he called a "woman's touch." Needlepoint and lace doilies were not for her. She had assumed her husband would be happy when he found out all of the practical things she could do. This was the West. She'd thought men needed women who could settle the land with them. She wasn't even sure she could tie the ribbon into a pretty bow.

She forced herself to stand tall and remember that she had no need to be ashamed.

If she were applying for a job here, she'd mention that she'd gotten quite a reputation on Nantucket Island for being able to sheer a sheep and, black or white, cord and weave its fleece into some of the softest flannel around. And, with the wool that was left, she could make beautiful dyed threads using onion peels or goldenrod flowers or even tree bark if that's all she had. Added to that, she knew herbs and salves well enough to cure whatever plagued a farm animal.

Any farmer should be happy to have her as his wife.

Given all of the confusion lately, though, she realized she had one critical question she had yet to ask. "You are planning to farm, aren't you? Cows and maybe some sheep? Mrs. Stout seemed to think—" she let her words trail away when she saw the scowl settle on his face.

Adam wondered what his mother had told Mrs. Stout and Eleanor. He'd only sent the one letter, but his mother had written one, or maybe two, before that. He hadn't even read what she'd said.

"You'll have enough to worry about with Hannah and the house." He realized he should have made it clear to the woman that he expected to make her life easier. "I'm not marrying you in hopes of having a field hand."

"Oh," she said.

He thought he saw something go out of her face, but it couldn't be. All of the women he knew would be happy to be spared a man's work. "I could probably use some help with the chickens if I can find someone willing to sell me a sitting hen."

She raised her head to him at that. "You can't mean to get one now. Baby chickens would freeze to death around here. I wouldn't even let my kitten outside at night. The wind comes from the north, down from Canada, right between those low mountains behind us. I've never felt anything so cold in my life. I can't imagine what a little chicken would do."

Her look demanded an answer.

"I plan to build a place for the hens to roost in a corner of the shelter. That backs up to the fireplace," he told her. He noticed she wasn't giving up anything, not even that cat. "They'll be warm enough there when we start to have a fire in the cabin more regularly—which we'll do from tonight on."

She nodded, but still seemed dubious. "You'll have to make the shed back there bigger. You'll keep the horses, of course, and we might want a cow. And maybe a few sheep."

"Whoa," Adam said. He'd been around this area long enough to know one thing. "This is going to be cattle country. There might not be many herds here yet, but none of our neighbors will speak to us if we bring in sheep. They eat the grass right down to the root. I know the Hargroves are bringing in more cattle from Texas this spring. Longhorns, I think."

"There's nothing wrong with sheep no matter how they eat their grass. The Good Lord Himself compared us to them. And we're His beloved children."

Unfortunately, his mother came through the curtain in time to hear Eleanor's defense of the wooly animals.

"You're not telling people you're Irish, are you?"

his mother demanded as she strode into the room with enough force to make a squadron hesitate. "All this foolishness about sheep. That's your father talking. Your mother was pure English—whether she talked to her parents or not, she had their blood, and hers is stronger than some poor Irishman's. That's all people need to know."

"What's that got to do with—" Adam began.

"I'm Irish enough," Eleanor said before he could even finish his words. She was squared off against his mother. "And I see no shame in it. Saint Patrick himself came to the blessed island and—"

"Hush, now. Surely, you don't want people to know," his mother continued as she reached up to tidy her hair. "You're in America now. You can see how people feel about the Irish. Putting aside their loud ways and fondness for strong drink, none of them are, well, refined enough for society. Think of the troubles it might cause Hannah."

"It's got nothing to do with Hannah," Adam protested.

"Well, of course not," Eleanor said as she turned away from him and walked toward the door.

She caught him by surprise and he said the first thing that occurred to him. "Stop. You can't go out there."

She turned around and looked at him. "Is that an order, Sergeant?"

"I'm out of the army now. Call me Adam," he commanded. "And it's bitter cold out there."

Her green eyes smoldered but she listened, so he

added, "The sun's almost gone down and you'll freeze. You don't even have a cloak with you. Where is your cloak, anyway?"

"I don't need one."

The fool woman was worried about unborn chickens and didn't have sense enough to take care of herself, he thought. And then he finally understood. "Surely, you have a cloak."

"I wrap up in a piece of my flannel. Or one of the army blankets. That works fine," she said and went over to sit down on the stool next to a ball of yarn. She picked up her knitting needles and began to knit something yellow.

"Nice yarn," he said by way of showing he was sorry he'd pricked her pride. He'd had no idea she wasn't properly provided for on that estate where she worked. Now wasn't the time to ask about it, though.

"I corded the yarn myself," she said, her voice not much warmer than before. But then she seemed to remember something and her mouth twisted. "Made a mistake by boiling it with some late-blooming goldenrods, though. It had been dry that year and the color didn't take for some reason. Mrs. Stout said the yellow was so faded and uneven it wasn't fit to warm the feet of the stable boy."

She looked at him, then. "You see, each year for Boxing Day the housemaids would knit a new pair of stockings for everyone on the estate. Since they couldn't use it, Mrs. Stout gave the yarn to me when I left. She said there'd be some use for it out West. Just like there'd be for me."

With that, she bent to her knitting and was silent.

"You miss the Stout estate?" he asked, unwilling to let the conversation die and still curious about how she'd fared there.

She nodded.

The sergeant was congratulating himself on making progress with his intended, when he heard a gasp behind him.

His mother had come into the room and was staring at the ceiling. "Whatever is that?"

Drops of mud were falling down onto the old piece of carpet that covered most of the packed dirt floor. It looked like several lengths of muslin had been nailed into place from beam to beam to cover the sod ceiling, but the material had obviously gotten damp and rotted.

"It's the snow on the roof," Eleanor said. "The fire must be warming things up."

"I'll go out and brush the snow off in a minute," he said.

"Hannah can't stay here," his mother said more quietly than he would have expected. She almost sounded as if she regretted the fact.

Adam didn't want to upset his mother, but he was going to keep his daughter with him.

"We'll fix this place," he assured her. "And, it's only for the winter. Come spring, I'll build us a new house. With sawmill planks and a roof that's not covered with sod. Hannah will do fine until then."

He glanced over to Eleanor and was surprised at the look of sympathy on her face.

"Here." She gathered her yarn and stood, gesturing for his mother to sit on the stool. "Mrs. Martin, please, sit here for a spell and I'll get supper on the table."

His mother nodded and walked over to the stool, sinking down on it as if she had more trouble than her heart could bear. Adam figured that's about how she felt, but he didn't risk asking her if everything was all right. He knew the list of things lacking in him and his home was long, and she'd name every one of them if he let her.

"I hope you're not planning to build another two-story house," his mother finally said, her voice clipped and her mouth firm. She was talking to him, but staring at Eleanor who had made her way over to the cook stove.

"No." He swallowed, and then managed to walk to the door. "It won't be that kind of a house. Not again."

He kept his back straight. His mother never hesitated to attack where he was most vulnerable. He was known for strategy when it came to leading troops into battle, but he had never found the way of anticipating her words. And she was right. He should have been able to muster a better plan for providing for his new wife.

The sting of icy air hit his face as he opened the door. When he married Eleanor, he would be pledging to care for and protect her. He didn't take that vow lightly. The gray sky had almost disappeared in the whiteness of the blizzard that was swirling around. Women, wives in particular, were such delicate creatures.

He needed to get the horses settled in the shelter for the night and then brush off the roof. The snow was wet and falling heavy by the time he got to the wagon. The contents that were still packed would be fine if he pulled the canvas tight over them and moved the wagon so it was sheltered by the cabin.

He did that and then fought the wind as he un-hitched the horses, all of which left his mind free to re-member things he'd sooner forget. He'd already failed to protect one wife. He remembered the house fire had come up while he had been out on patrol almost a year ago. Catherine had wanted to live away from the fort so there was only one neighbor, a frail man, who was around to come to their rescue. The flames had al-ready touched Catherine and their daughter when his panicked wife managed to toss Hannah out of their upstairs window, no doubt hoping the girl would fall into the arms of the neighbor who stood below call-ing out to them. The old man was not strong enough to catch her right, though, and his daughter injured the same leg that had been scorched in the blaze.

In all the terror of that, his wife became increas-ingly agitated and finally refused to jump, saying she was too afraid. Adam lived with the knowledge that, if he'd been there, he would have saved them both. A sergeant's first duty was to the ones under his care and he'd failed to be there when they needed him the most.

He'd given up asking God to forgive him. It was his fault his wife died; he deserved any suffering he had. She had hated military life and had begged him to let her father set him up with a desk job in Washington. She complained that life was too difficult in the West and she wanted the parties she used to attend in the capital. He told her he'd be stifled behind a desk. She refused to hear his reasons, retreating into the vapid conversation that had characterized their courtship, and eventually he hadn't known what to do but agree to ask her father. He was too late, though. If he had heeded her desires when she first voiced them, she would be alive today.

He shoved his memories aside. Even if he hadn't given up the army for Catherine, he had no choice but to do so for Hannah. Now that his daughter had been scarred and crippled, she was even more delicate than his wife had been. She needed him and he did not intend to be absent again.

After he settled the horses into the shelter and gave them some of the hay that was stacked along one wall, he took a shovel outside and scraped the sides of the roof. The movement was enough to make the snow tumble down to the ground.

He'd taken off his gloves before feeding the horses and his hands were red and damp after moving the snow so he quickly walked back to get them before returning to the wagon. He uncovered a saddle bag from the back, rummaging through it to find the utensils he'd used at the fort. He'd always considered himself well supplied because he had two tin spoons for eating and the same number of cups for coffee.

The wind was loud and strong as he put the utensils inside his coat and fought his way back to the cabin.

He opened the door and then closed it, only to have the noise stilled once he was inside. The place was stronger than he'd thought since it didn't rattle.

"The drip stopped," Eleanor informed him when he walked through the door.

"Good."

He brought the cups and spoons out from inside his coat and set them down on the split-log table in the cabin. It was clear they weren't enough. The trapper hadn't left anything that could be used for eating. Eleanor had a bent spoon and a chipped china plate that she credited her employer with giving her on some Christmas years ago.

"We'll have to share," Adam said, too tired to make it sound any better than it was.

Fortunately, his mother didn't protest. She was sitting on one of Hannah's trunks and his daughter was seated on the stool.

Eleanor took the cast-iron skillet over to the table and served his mother on the plate before giving Hannah a cup of beans.

Then Eleanor silently filled the other cup and held it out to him.

It was a simple gesture, but it brought a lump to his throat. He had always been the one to do for Catherine. Neither of them had expected her to sacrifice more for him than she had when she married him.

"You eat," he said to Eleanor with a shake of his head. "I should get some more wood before it gets too dark, anyway."

She looked at him for a long moment, and then

nodded. She gingerly sat down on the other half of the trunk that held his mother. The flame in the fireplace gave a golden light to the room and he noticed she'd pulled her bright hair back into a tidy bun. He rather missed the abundance of her hair when it was loose.

"I'll bring the buffalo robe inside," he said as he stood beside the table. Having announced he'd get the wood, he found himself reluctant to leave. "I'll bed down with the horses tonight. There's some hay in the corner of the shelter."

"I figured your mother and Hannah could share the bed," Eleanor said with a glance at the other woman. "I don't mind sleeping out here by the fire."

"That's kind of you," his mother said with a congenial nod, and then spoiled it by adding, "Hannah isn't used to sharing a room with strangers."

"Eleanor's not a stranger, Mother," Adam said, and then to reinforce his words he turned to Eleanor. "We'll ask to see the reverend tomorrow when we go into Miles City."

Adam was surprised to see a pink blush cover the woman's face. She suddenly looked very young so he added, "If that's all right with you?"

He was bungling things already. Maybe he was supposed to formally ask for her hand in marriage again. He should have paid more attention when his mother talked about these arrangements.

Eleanor seemed uncertain for a moment and then stiffened. "Yes. Tomorrow is fine."

Her green eyes filled with resolve until she looked as if she was facing a firing squad without the benefit of a blindfold. Her back was rigid and her shoulders square.

"We could wait a few days," he offered. "As long as my mother is here, it's proper."

That would give him time to buy her some candy or take her for a walk in the moonlight. Except that it was freezing outside and all the mercantile in Miles City had was licorice and penny candy. A woman like Eleanor deserved a tin of those fancy chocolates that came over by ship from France. They had to be brought overland to the territories from Seattle, though, and not many tins made it through.

"I'd just as soon do it quick," Eleanor said, looking straight ahead and not meeting his eyes. "The getting married part, that is."

He heard his mother shift on the trunk. "Goodness. There's no need to rush anything. Why, you've only just met each other." Then she turned to look at his future wife. "I could always pay your way home, dear. I'm sure Mrs. Stout would take you back, even with the nephew there. She spoke so highly of you in her letters."

"Mother—" he warned.

He suddenly noticed his daughter was on the verge of tears.

"But Hannah—" the woman managed to say with a glance at his daughter. She must have seen the look on his daughter's face, too.

"Don't worry. Hannah can just come back with me," his mother said, looking at him defiantly. "We can't have her raised by this sheep woman. With me, she will learn to be a lady. We need to just forget all this marriage nonsense and go back to the way it was."

"It's not your decision," Adam said more harshly than he intended. He realized in some surprise that it wasn't just for Hannah. He didn't want the woman to go back, either.

Then a quiet sob escaped his daughter.

Eleanor reached a hand across the table and covered Hannah's small one with her own. The woman and his daughter looked at each other and smiled.

"Tomorrow will be fine for the wedding," Eleanor finally said quietly.

"Good." He nodded even though he realized what he'd seen. The woman was staying for his daughter's sake. He told himself it was for the best, that this is what he had wanted. There was no reason for him to feel disappointed.

Suddenly, he wished he had met this fine woman years ago when he could have courted her properly. He used to have a reputation for being a smooth dancer and witty enough to be sought after in society. Of course, that was before he'd joined the army. And gotten married and become a widower. So much had happened since then, he wasn't sure he remembered how to be charming anymore.

"I should go get that buffalo robe," he said finally, turning to leave.

"If you bring in the wood, I'll see that the fire keeps going all night," Eleanor offered as she looked up at him. "You'll be warm enough if you bed down on the back side of the fireplace."

He nodded as he walked to the door. The sooner everyone went to bed, the earlier they would get up in the morning and make their way into Miles City. He'd need to unload the wagon so they'd have room to bring back all of the supplies they needed.

Suddenly, he wondered if they had any silk ribbons at the mercantile he could buy for Eleanor's hair. He'd like long ones so she could tie it back loosely enough so the curls would be free. He didn't want to see any part of her restrained.

Chapter Three

In the darkness, Eleanor stood by the fireplace and pulled the army blanket closer around her shoulders. Even though the sound of the wind outside had disappeared, it was still chilly. Everyone had gone to bed and the fire had died down. She had risen to add more wood, and then watched the embers flare up as the blaze took hold again. The truth was she hadn't been able to sleep.

Every time she had closed her eyes, she remembered that tomorrow was going to be her wedding day. She'd had months to get used to the idea, but it seemed a lot more difficult than she had thought it was going to be when she was talking to Mrs. Stout about the comforts of being married as they sat at the worktable back in Nantucket and planned her future.

Frankly, nothing her employer had said to her in those conversations prepared her for marrying a man like the sergeant. No, Adam—he said to call him Adam—she reminded herself as she reached up and brushed the hair away from her face. She could do that, she reassured herself. Adam. That was simple enough.

He was nothing like the men she'd known back home.

The buffalo robe lay on the floor and she told herself she should lie back down and try to sleep. Couples got married every day of the week and, while not all of those unions were based on love, people managed to have quiet, contented lives. The kind of life she'd had with her father as they cared for the sheep. The kind of life she had expected when Mrs. Stout first told her about Adam.

Maybe that was the problem, she told herself as she looked into the flames. Somehow she didn't think a marriage with Adam would be as steady as she had imagined. He certainly didn't like sheep and that was one mark against him. And he was too handsome by half. She couldn't figure out why he was settling for a bride he didn't know when he could just walk down the street of the nearest town and find a woman who'd beg to be his wife.

That's what he should have done. At least, Adam and whoever he chose would get to talk to each other before deciding to spend their lives together. Not that she liked that idea so much, either, once she'd thought of it.

Just then she heard a slight sound and looked up to see Mrs. Martin come out of the back room with her thick shawl clutched tight over her linen shift and her hair carefully tucked under a white sleeping cap. She wore stockings on her feet and the night shadows on her face hid her expression.

Eleanor could imagine how she felt, though. "It's a big day tomorrow. I guess we all have problems going to sleep."

"Hannah snuck that cat into the room and it climbed up on the bed with us," Mrs. Martin said accusingly.

"It's only a kitten."

The other woman didn't answer. Eleanor was almost going to offer to boil some hot water for them both. She didn't have tea, but she'd brought some dried rose hips with her that she could add to the water to make it more soothing. After all, this woman was Adam's mother and Hannah's grandmother. Eleanor needed to make an effort to get along with her for their sakes.

The older woman stood still, and then straightened herself as if she had something to say, clearing her throat and paused for a moment before beginning. "I'm prepared to pay your train fare back to the East Coast," Mrs. Martin finally said in even tones that suggested she'd practiced the words enough in her mind that they seemed reasonable.

Then she took a breath.

"And I'll give you a hundred dollars in addition for your trouble. That's more than fair," she added as though she expected some argument on that point. "Especially when we both know that, even with the nephew, Mrs. Stout will let you return to her estate and a shepherd wouldn't make that much all year if you'd stayed there, anyway. I can't imagine who would want to take care of those smelly beasts, but it is not a difficult thing, now is it?"

Eleanor was silent for a moment, striving for patience. "I know I'm not who you wanted or expected me to be, but I promise you I'll do the best I can for Hannah. I have a book that Mrs. Stout gave me and—"

"Don't be ridiculous," the older woman snapped, obviously annoyed. "You can't teach someone how to be a lady from some book. Or be one yourself, for that matter. There are so many things. It takes training. Why—you need to show Hannah how be a hostess. Have you thought of that? You've certainly never done anything like that. Adam will be an important man someday. There will be dinners. And parties."

The woman paused, and then continued, "I'm afraid Adam just doesn't understand how difficult that can be for someone who wasn't raised to handle themselves in any kind of society. If he knew you better, he'd see it's just not possible. I'm sure you do fine with the sheep, but you need to be able to converse with people if you're married to a man like Adam."

Eleanor was taken back at the disdain in the older woman's voice. "Mrs. Martin, I assure you I don't just talk to sheep."

But the other woman wasn't listening. She had let go of her shawl and now held out her hand, causing the garment to fall slightly until it rested softly upon her shoulders. In her palm she held a small tintype of a woman, set in a delicate silver frame. "This was my son's first wife, Catherine, at their engagement ball."

Mrs. Martin spoke softly, lost in some memory as she looked down at the portrait.

Eleanor stepped closer so she could see. Maybe if she showed she was interested that would be taken as a sign of friendship. She didn't realize she was holding her breath until she needed to exhale.

So that's why Mrs. Martin was upset, she thought to herself as she fought the temptation to turn her head away. Hannah's mother—Adam's wife—had been absolutely beautiful. She had her dark hair arranged in an intricate knot that Eleanor would never have been able to manage with her thick tresses. And then she wore a gown that showed off her sleek neck and the pearl necklace that encircled it so casually that it was clear that she belonged to a world where those were commonplace. It was the smile on her face as she looked up at someone to the side of her that made Eleanor stop cold, though. Whoever she was looking at, Catherine loved him with all her heart.

"She and Adam danced perfectly together," his mother continued, studying the portrait as if she was willing past events to come back to life. "People loved to watch them. They were so very graceful, like the swans on her parent's estate as they glided across the pond. I haven't seen Adam dance like that since. I don't think he could bear to even try it now. Those days are over for him."

Eleanor swallowed the lump in her throat and searched for something to say. It was clear that Catherine had been perfect.

"She was rich?" Eleanor finally asked, for lack of

anything else to say. She knew that money wasn't the reason for that engagement, though. She wished it had been.

"Yes, far more than we were. Her father tried to dissuade her from marrying Adam. But then he decided my son had prospects, after all, and, for the sake of Catherine's happiness, he relented and agreed they could wed. He expected great things of their life together."

Eleanor nodded, unable to speak.

They were silent for a moment and then the woman continued, "It's for Catherine's sake that Hannah needs to have a proper upbringing." She finally looked at Eleanor. The fierceness had disappeared and she seemed to be pleading for something. "Surely, you understand. Some day her mother's parents are going to want Hannah to come visit them. She needs to prepare for that day. She and Adam will go to her grandparent's home, either in the capital city or beside the bay. Neither one of them will want to lack manners or polish on that day."

For a moment, Eleanor was reminded of her own situation. What if she was in Hannah's position and had been given that coveted invitation? Even with all of her bitterness, she would go. Maybe her mother's parents had never made any effort to meet her because they felt she would not know how to act in their world. She was used to their indifference, but she felt an unexpected sharp jab of rejection at the thought they might be worried about her manners. No one liked to be cast aside because they weren't good enough.

"Hasn't she seen her grandparents?" Eleanor couldn't help but ask. Maybe Mrs. Martin was exaggerating.

"Not since her mother died."

Eleanor's heart sank as she stood there looking at the picture, and then remembered the little girl sleeping in the other room.

It was a mercy, she told herself stoically, that she had never expected a love match with the sergeant. No man would ever love again after being wed to Catherine. Whatever he was doing now was for the sake of his daughter and Eleanor didn't have the heart to fault him for that.

"Hannah has her mother's eyes," Mrs. Martin murmured, and then looked up at Eleanor. "I know it sounds harsh. But it's the only way. Please think about my offer."

Eleanor nodded. She could barely speak, but she needed to hear the truth. "Does your son know what you're asking me to do?"

"No, but—" The other woman didn't finish her thought. She didn't need to. Once Eleanor had seen the portrait, she knew she wasn't like his late wife. She was a shepherd's daughter. She had no desire to make Adam miserable by marrying him. She'd assumed when he sent for a bride that he was willing to make a life with whoever answered—that his heart was open to accept anyone. But maybe it was the opposite; maybe he wasn't planning to open his heart to anyone so it didn't matter who he married. Maybe that's why he hadn't bothered to prepare himself, or this cabin, for their life together.

"There's no need to tell Adam about our talk," his mother finally finished. "Just make some excuse to delay the marriage. I don't want to spoil Christmas for Hannah. She is so excited to be here with her father. It's only two days. You can tell them after Christmas. It will come soon enough."

"How can I leave if Hannah wants me to stay?"

The man might not care if she left, but she believed his daughter would.

"A child shouldn't make those kinds of decisions. You know that. I never wanted Hannah to leave Ohio, anyway. She belongs with me and I'll take her back home."

"But Adam—"

"My son will do his duty once you go back. He doesn't realize how frail Hannah is. Her scars won't fade. And her leg hasn't recovered from that fall. He has completely unrealistic expectations of her becoming a normal girl someday. And he can't take care of her alone. She needs someone with her. She needs me."

Eleanor was suddenly very tired. She turned to walk back to the fireplace and didn't look at the other woman when she spoke. "Morning will come early. We should both get some rest."

Eleanor didn't wait for the older woman's footsteps to end before lying down on the buffalo robe and drawing it around her for warmth. She was so very cold. *Please, Lord,* she prayed. *Help me know what to do.*

She had no wish for Hannah to experience the rejection she had felt from her mother's family. Would she be able to learn enough to prepare Hannah for the expectations of her grandparents? The book Mrs. Stout had sent with her was in her valise in the bedroom; she wished she had thought to bring the bag out here so she could look at it now.

The book was written by Emily Thornwell and called *Good Manners for Young Ladies.* Eleanor wondered if Adam's mother was right that she wouldn't find enough in its pages to help her and Hannah. If she hadn't been so busy making the yarn stars, she would have read the book by now and she might know if it held any hope.

And then there's Adam, Eleanor thought as she bowed her head again. *Lord, what should I do about him?* He was still grieving for his wife. He probably always would be. No one had given her any advice on how to live with a husband who was in love with someone else. *Lord, why have You brought me here?*

The house quieted again until she knew Mrs. Martin and Hannah were both asleep. Even prayer did not soothe Eleanor tonight. God seemed far away. Of course, He never seemed as close to her as He did when she could see the stars.

She glanced up at the window. The clouds had shifted and the sky looked clear. There was no wind blowing and the snow had stopped falling.

She looked over at the fire. The embers were still

red and a low steady heat was coming from the pile of white ashes under them. She needed to get up and put more wood in the fire again, anyway, she told herself as she stood and quietly put on her dress. She carried the stool and the rest of her clothes over to the door, sitting down to put her shoes on when she got there.

A blanket hung from a peg on the wall and she wrapped that around herself before quietly unlatching the door and stepping outside. The air was cold, but it didn't sting like it had earlier. She pulled the blanket closer to her, crossing her arms in front of her as she did so. The snow that had fallen earlier was soft as she took a few steps away from the house and looked back at it.

She might not feel as if she belonged inside that cabin, but no such discomfort plagued her when she was able to go outside like this in the evenings. The land was flat in all directions, but the depth of the night skies took her breath away. She should be used to it since she'd come out on other nights to look through her father's telescope. The stars were in different places here than they had been when she studied them in the sheep's commons back home, but she couldn't deny that they were more magnificent.

She walked a little farther from the cabin. The moon was shining tonight, giving a silver glow to the snowy ground. She wondered briefly who would live in the cabin if Mrs. Martin took Hannah back East with her. Eleanor knew that without Hannah the sergeant would have no reason to marry. Nor would he have anything preventing him from going back to the fort and taking up his old life. She felt lonely just thinking about it. She wondered if the man would let her buy the cabin from him if he left. She couldn't pay him until she raised a crop on the land this spring, but she was strong and could manage. She did have enough money from her savings to start a small herd of sheep, too. She might be able to sell some wool.

She would never consider taking the railroad fare or the payment Mrs. Martin would press on her. Contrary to what the other woman thought, Eleanor knew the nephew made a difference. He had probably already moved into the main house by now. Some of the other staff members were likely being told to leave about now, as well. Mrs. Stout had a kind heart, but it was said her husband's nephew didn't.

Eleanor heard something behind her and spun around.

"Oh," she breathed out.

"Sorry. I should have said something earlier." Adam was heading toward her. "You just looked so deep in thought that I didn't want to disturb you at first. Then I thought you might want this."

He held out another blanket.

Eleanor was dumbstruck. The man was handsome in daylight, but in the light of the moon he stirred something deep inside her. Maybe it was the way the shadows defined his face, bringing out the sculpted look of his strong bones. She remembered the legends her father used to tell about the Norsemen of old who were fiercely protective and kind to those they loved.

Adam could have sprung to life from those stories, especially with the caring look in his eyes.

"I know you have something around your shoulders, but if it's one of the blankets that came with the cabin, I've noticed they aren't as warm as they could be. This one is almost new."

His voice was soothing and he walked even closer, opening the blanket as he came.

Finally, he stood in front of her and wrapped the covering around her, letting his arms linger as he held her shoulders. "I couldn't sleep, either. I hope you're not nervous."

Eleanor shook her head as she gazed up at him. She was not used to men who were as tall as he was. "No, that's not it. I'm just tired so I came out here to pray."

She wondered if he could see the hesitation on her face as she stood there. He'd moved and his eyes were in the shadows of his face now, but she could see from the tiny wrinkles around them that he was smiling.

"All the more reason to get some rest, then," he said softly. "That is, if you've finished your prayers?"

She nodded.

She had not given much thought until now to how nice his voice sounded. It had a small lilt to it that she hadn't noticed before. He was pleasing to the ear as well as the eye.

"You grew up in Ohio?" she asked, wondering if that was what gave him the smooth tones.

"I forget you don't know much about me," he replied with a slow nod.

They were silent for a moment, neither moving even

though a fine mist of snow had started falling on them. Eleanor felt it on her face, but it wasn't cold like it had been earlier. She hadn't given the stars another thought since Adam had come to stand in front of her. Maybe the warmth she was feeling came from him? she wondered. She knew it wasn't just the blankets.

"You're a courageous woman," he said as he reached out his hand and brushed the melted snow off of her cheek. "Marrying a stranger like me."

She felt herself blush. She wasn't used to compliments.

And then he cupped her cheek and rubbed his thumb across her skin. "Beautiful, too."

She stepped back and shook her head. "My hair is bright as brass, and I'm too large."

"Oh?" he said with a frown.

She nodded emphatically. "Men like little women. I'm too tall and filled out."

At that he chuckled quietly. "I happen to like my woman tall and, as you say, filled out."

"No, you don't," she said without thinking. She wasn't supposed to know what kind of women he liked, but she did. She'd seen the woman's face in the tintype. Catherine had been slight and fragile, a true lady's dream.

The cold came between them until, even with the extra blanket, Eleanor started to shiver. She moved to step around Adam so she could go back to the house, but he put a hand out to stop her.

"I want you to know I intend to be a good husband

to you," he said, his voice deep and raspy. "You don't need to lose sleep worrying about me."

"I—" Eleanor began and stopped. She couldn't tell him what was troubling her. Not when he was looking at her so seriously. So she nodded.

Then he cupped her chin again and tilted her face up to him.

"I'll always think of you in the moonlight," he said, and then he kissed her.

Eleanor thought her heart would stop as his lips pressed lightly to hers. But it was nothing, she tried to convince herself. It was just that the kiss was unexpected.

When Adam lifted his head, she couldn't think what to say, but she opened her mouth, anyway. "I've been kissed before."

"Oh?" he asked.

She nodded. "He was one of the groomsmen on the estate. He walked with me in the gardens one night so I could tell him about the stars."

"I see," Adam added.

"It was nothing like this," Eleanor said, her misery shining through in her words, and turned to go back to the house. This time he didn't stop her, and she walked as fast as she could because she didn't want him to know that tears were streaming down her cheeks.

Lord, what have I done? she prayed as she opened the door and slipped back into the cabin. *I'm not supposed to care about him. The marriage was only to be for Hannah's sake. I can't possibly want to be his wife for my sake.*

* * *

Adam stood in the moonlight and wondered what he had done wrong. Unless he was mistaken, he had seen the glisten of tears in Eleanor's eyes before she rushed off. He'd been surprised when he'd heard someone leave the cabin, because he knew it had to be her. The fact that she was restless, no doubt because she was going to marry him tomorrow, reminded him of how solemn the vows were that they were going to take.

They were pledging to be a family together, to work and make a life here on this land.

He never meant to kiss her, though. That had been an impulse, and he didn't usually give in to those. He hadn't expected the open sweetness that shone out of Eleanor. He'd noticed it earlier, but as she stood there looking up at the skies it became enticing. It didn't make any sense, really. She just seemed more alive than most people.

He thought about it a moment and decided that was it. He was used to women who kept their emotions hidden, wearing polite faces of interest even when listening to the dullest of topics and showing only tepid enjoyment in everything else. Their laughter was staged as often as not and a man never knew what these ladies thought. It had certainly been true of Catherine, anyway. But there was nothing hidden or subdued about Eleanor.

She was, in fact, more vibrant than he was.

He had the uneasy feeling that she might expect more from him in marriage than he had the heart to give. What did a man do when he was a burned-out husk who couldn't risk loving someone again?

It wasn't the fire that had shown him what kind of a man he was, either. It had come to him with the slowly growing coldness that had entered his marriage long before the fire ever happened. There wasn't a specific day, but he remembered glimpses of unease until he finally realized that Catherine was play-acting around him. She might be herself with other people, but not with him.

Some days he had longed for a friend to sit down and talk with, but she would get up and leave the room if he said anything serious. The only thing she seemed to want was for him to play the beau unceasingly, flirting and talking nonsense. He wondered at times why he hadn't noticed that they had never talked about anything of substance when they had been courting.

Remembering, though, made Eleanor seem suddenly precious to him.

With one last look up at the stars, he walked back to the shelter and settled down on his bed of hay. Tomorrow would come soon enough, he thought as he remembered that Eleanor had gone outside, probably to pray her way past her nervousness. He used to turn to God with his troubles, but it seemed a long time ago. He wondered if he'd ever have that kind of faith again. Maybe tomorrow, when he spoke to the reverend, he would ask if there was hope for a man like him. He'd like to feel God's presence the way he used to when he had been young.

He lay there for a time and then, just before he

drifted off to sleep, he heard the faint sound of wood being placed onto the fire on the other side of the wall. He put his hand up and felt the warm rocks that formed the back of the fireplace and it comforted him. Eleanor was remembering her promise to keep the fire going for him. Well, he chuckled, for him and the horses, no doubt. She did seem to love animals.

Chapter Four

It was barely light when a noise woke Adam abruptly the next morning. He reached for his rifle, thinking he was still sleeping on the flat windswept prairie with his troops. Then he realized that, even though the packed dirt beneath him was cold enough to be outside, he could actually see walls around him. The shadows in the place took shape until he saw his two horses standing in a crude stall on the other side of the structure. The animals must have awakened him, he thought as he rolled over. The dried hay he'd bedded down in last night shifted as he moved and gave off a fine dust that made him cough.

He sat up and ran his fingers through his hair to dislodge any pieces of hay. Then he felt his hair again to be sure it was all gone. No woman, he told himself with a grin, wanted to marry a man with straw in his hair. Not even a woman who liked animals as much as Eleanor apparently did.

He looked around more as he savored the fact that

this was his wedding day. When he first set up the arrangement, he'd seen it as a practical solution to his problem of caring for Hannah. But after meeting Eleanor, he knew the union might hold joy for him, too.

So, he told himself, it was fitting that he woke up to meet the dawn. The subdued light was coming through the logs where the chinking had worn away. Then he noticed that snow was coming inside along with it. A few inches had even settled along the wide crack under the door. He had a lot of work to do before this place was snug. He suspected his new wife would insist he work on the animal's shelter before he worried about the house itself, he thought with a grin.

Suddenly, he became aware of the strength of the wind and stood up, intending to crack the door open so he could see how bad the storm was. He had barely swung it an inch outward when a bitter cold gust blew at him, almost pressing the door closed again. He had to stand with his shoulders braced to keep it open. As dark as it was inside the shelter, everything outside was startling white. And the snow felt like ice as it beat against his face as he stood there, looking out at the landscape.

When he saw the depth of the snow and the ferocity of the storm, his heart sank. All the plans he had made for them to go to Miles City today disappeared. No one was going to be able to travel anywhere in this weather, especially not in an open wagon. He'd had disappointing days before, but none like this.

He hoped his bride was as faithful to God as she seemed to be. Many women, who did not believe God controlled such matters as the weather, would say the storm was an omen that meant the marriage they'd planned for that day was doomed. It didn't always take much to turn a woman against a man, and Eleanor had only met him yesterday. He didn't know what he would do if she decided to go back home to Mrs. Stout and her sheep. Hopefully, Eleanor could understand that the weather was only a temporary delay.

Please, Lord, he said in a tentative prayer. It had been a long time since he'd talked to God and he was hesitant to do so now. This was important, though. *I have no right to ask, but could You make Eleanor happy to stay?*

He was trying to think of what else he should add to his prayer when he heard a sound in the distant swirling blizzard. He cocked his head so he could listen more closely. He thought it was a horse's neigh, but there were no neighbors near enough for him to hear their animals. Squinting into the wind, he struggled to see what was out there. It wasn't until one of his horses answered the call that Adam knew he hadn't imagined the sound. Someone was riding a horse close by—even though, to his experienced eye, only a fool would travel in a blizzard like this.

He closed the door and hurried to put his boots on so he could find out who was coming. Whoever they were, they must need help. He didn't know what else would compel a man to venture forth in this kind of weather. He stood before the door a second time and braced himself. Even with that, the force of the wind almost blew the door off its leather hinges before he was able to step out and close it again.

As he turned the corner, he could see the dark shape of a rider on a horse moving slowly toward the house. Adam fought to walk to the door of the house, and then he pounded so he could be heard inside. The horse and rider came closer and he relaxed. The man out in this weather was a fool all right. He smiled as he recognized his neighbor, Jake Hargrove.

Adam was ready to knock again when he heard the latch slide and the door move slightly. When he looked down, Eleanor was peering through the small slit in the door. He doubted she could see out into the snow any more than he had been able to earlier.

"We've got a visitor," he yelled through the opening, hoping she could hear above the sound of the storm. "I'll stay out and take care of his horse. I just wanted you to know so you're—"

He could see by both the blush on her cheeks and what little of her pink dress that was visible through the slit in the door that she was ready for company, so he didn't go further.

By that time, Jake was sliding off his horse. The man had a cut-off piece of blanket wrapped around his ears and a Stetson hat pushed down to cover everything, but ice had still crusted in his beard and snow had fallen on the shoulders of his buckskin jacket even with a buffalo robe wrapped around him.

"You're a sight for sore eyes," Jake said as he held out his hand. "It's about time you got home so you can marry this new bride of yours."

Adam smiled as he shook the man's hand and then held out his other hand to take the reins of the horse. "I'll walk him around back and feed him some oats. You just go on in and get warm."

Jake nodded and turned to the house. Eleanor had been waiting and opened the door enough for him to slip through.

"Come along, old boy," Adam said as he tugged on the reins and started to lead the horse around the corner so they could go inside the shelter.

It didn't take long for Adam to rub the horse down and give it some of the hay that he'd used for his bed last night. Then he gave all of the horses some oats. Fortunately, he'd brought a good supply of feed out in the wagon with him because he hadn't ordered that from the mercantile. Later this morning, he'd melt some of the snow so the horses would have something fresh to drink. Either that or he'd have to take that bucket down to the creek and chop a hole in the ice to find water.

The horses were eating contentedly as he slipped out the door. The wind seemed to have died down some because he could see more clearly. He followed the sides of the house until he could reach out and knock.

Eleanor opened the door enough for him to enter, all the while keeping it partially closed to preserve the heat inside. The warmth made his fingers tingle as he took off his gloves and walked farther into the room. The air was damp, but he realized it was from the steam rising from the kettle on the cook stove.

The window was frosted and not much light came through, but the fireplace gave off a soft glow that lit the cabin well enough.

"Would you like something hot to drink?" Eleanor asked as she gestured to the table where Jake sat with one of the tin cups cradled in his hands. "You need to warm up."

"It smells good," he said in surprise. He had a bit of green coffee in his saddle bags, left over from the supplies he'd used when he'd been out on patrol. He should have brought it inside last night, but he'd bring it later. Eleanor clearly didn't need it now. He was curious about what she was serving.

"I packed some rose hips with me," Eleanor said as she walked over to the stove and poured some boiling water into the other tin cup. She then added something from a linen pouch. "It's not exactly tea, but it's good for you. I sometimes put hibiscus petals with it if I have any."

"I've already made her promise to tell Elizabeth how to make it," Jake said as he lifted his cup to take another drink. "I like it. Reminds me of something my father used to drink."

Adam nodded as he sat down on one of the trunks they were using for chairs by the table. It wasn't often that Jake mentioned either of his deceased parents. "Is everything okay over at your place?"

Jake grinned. "I told Elizabeth anyone who saw me out there today would be worried about that. No one with any sense goes out on a day like this, but Elizabeth kept fretting about Eleanor until I said I'd ride over and see her. My wife wanted me to bring her back to our place for Christmas, but now that you're all here, I can tell Elizabeth she won't be alone."

"That's kind of you," Adam said, a picture coming to his mind of how dreary it would have been for Eleanor if he hadn't been able to come home in time for the holiday.

"I appreciate it," he added to show how much he valued his friend's effort.

Of course, Jake knew how to survive worse storms than this one. He had been raised deep in the mountains west of here, staying with the Lakota Sioux part of the time, and he could hold his own in the winter. His wife was a nice, sensible woman, too, even though she'd come from the East. She wouldn't let him go out if she had any doubts he would return.

"Well, if it was up to Elizabeth, no one anywhere would be alone for Christmas," Jake said with a rueful shake of his head. "I tell her some folks like to spend the day with no one else around to pester them. They might enjoy some peace and quiet, I say. But she doesn't agree.

"She insisted I invite a couple of my trapper friends for dinner last Christmas," he continued fondly. "She wouldn't take no for an answer. I expected them to refuse, but they came and almost burst into tears like babies when she brought out the apple pie she'd made for dessert. They swore they'd died and gone to heaven when they took their first bite. She had to promise to make them another pie just to get them to leave. Now every time I see them they want some pie."

There was a rustle in the doorway between the two rooms and Adam looked up to see his mother push back the curtain and come out, fully dressed in her best maroon outfit and her hair twisted into a bun that he knew would accommodate one of those hats she liked to wear.

Adam stood at the same time his neighbor did. He was pleased that his mother had put on her church clothes; she must have assumed the trip into town was still the plan for the day. Her clothes were a mark of the respect she had for his wedding ceremony and that made him feel good. She had come around to his way of thinking it seemed. They all needed Eleanor.

"I'd like you to meet my mother," Adam said with a nod in the direction of the other man. "My daughter is probably still tucked under her blankets. They came in with me yesterday off the train and I'm afraid they're a bit worn out.

"Mother," he added with a smile to her. "This is our neighbor, Jake Hargrove. He and his wife have a couple of girls that Hannah will enjoy meeting and a little boy who was just learning to walk when I saw him last."

"Pleased to meet you, ma'am," Jake said as he walked over and offered his hand to Adam's mother. "All your son could talk about the last time we spent any time together was the fact that you were bringing his daughter home. I'm glad you both made it in time for Christmas."

"You're too kind," his mother said to the other man, but Adam noticed her jaw was clenched a little.

He supposed she was upset about the buckskins Jake wore. If Adam was not mistaken, before the day was over, she'd be scolding him because he let a man who wore heathen clothes come in and sit down at the table as if he belonged in their home.

"I worried, too," Adam said, and then trying to appease her, he added, "But my mother has been gracious in allowing Hannah to stay with her for too long now. I know it's been a lot of work for her and it's time I started doing it instead."

"Oh, it was nothing," his mother said with a wave of her hands. "I enjoy having our Hannah around. A little one like her still needs her grandmother."

"Well, my girls have been talking about getting to play with her for months now," Jake said as he turned to walk back to the table. He sat down and picked up his cup again. "They're going to wish they could have come with me to meet her today."

Adam took a long sip from his cup and studied his mother. Everything looked very proper on the surface, but something was still wrong. He just couldn't decide what it was. Surely his mother wasn't upset that Hannah would meet some other children. He knew one of the Hargrove girls must be quite a bit older than his daughter, but out here in the West children didn't separate by ages as much as they did back East. There weren't enough of them around to do that.

"You'll have to bring them over to meet Hannah," his mother said, some of the brooding lifting from her face. Then she glanced over at where Eleanor stood by the stove. "Wouldn't that be nice, Eleanor?"

"Lovely."

"We'll have a little party," his mother continued with more satisfaction in her voice than seemed justified.

"They'd like that," Jake agreed.

Adam decided he was being fanciful as he watched his mother. What harm could come with some little girls getting together for a party with his daughter?

"Why don't we do it for Christmas?" Adam heard his mother say. Her voice was melodic and calm. For a moment, he didn't realize even what she'd said. "Bring your whole family and come visit us."

"Tomorrow?" Jake asked, a little surprised.

"Bring your trapper friends, too, if they are at your place," his mother said with a smile. "We have room for everyone."

"Mother, we can't—" Adam began. What was wrong with her? She knew they only had three cups.

Jake responded in a friendly voice, "Now, ma'am, I know you just got here. And I'm thinking Eleanor probably wants to have some time to get to know all of you before you invite your neighbors over."

Adam continued to watch the smile broaden on his mother's face and he could see there was trouble coming.

"Eleanor would be delighted if you'd join us," his mother said as she turned to the other woman. "Wouldn't you, dear? It will be a chance for you to show Adam what kind of a hostess you are."

"Surely, there's no need," Adam tried again, but he realized his future bride wasn't listening to him.

Instead, her cheeks pinked up and she got a fire of some sort in her eyes. Then she looked at his mother in the way a new recruit looks at his first sergeant— a little fearful of what hurdle would be required but determined to do his best, anyway.

"I don't think—" Adam started, but his future bride interrupted before he could finish.

"It would be my pleasure," Eleanor said firmly and then she turned to face Jake. "I do hope you and your family can come over tomorrow. We'd enjoy your company."

Her voice was formal, but sincere.

"Well, if the snow calms down, maybe we can come for a short while," Jake said cautiously and then grinned. "The truth is, if I tell Elizabeth and the girls, they'll have the team all hitched up before breakfast regardless of what the weather is like. They've been inside for days now and they won't be able to resist meeting some new folks. We'll be here for a bit in the morning."

"But surely you'll stay for dinner. That's what you meant, isn't it, dear?" his mother asked as she turned to Eleanor.

Only his years of dealing with his mother revealed to Adam the slightly malicious edge to her voice.

That's when he remembered what very little food they had. How could he have forgotten? "I'm afraid it won't—"

A sharp glance from Eleanor stopped him. He knew from the pallor on her face that she was counting the cans of peaches that were left, as well, but for some reason she was not going to stop this. "We'll eat at noon. That way you'll have time to get back home before it gets dark."

If he didn't know better, Adam would think that his bride-to-be and his mother had just faced off against each other. He'd need to find out what was happening between them before there arose any resentful feeling that couldn't be calmed down. He looked at their faces and wondered if he wasn't already too late.

Eleanor watched as their visitor walked back to where he'd entered. Adam had to go over and pull the door closed after the man left so the wind wouldn't blow in more snow. The inside of the cabin had never been so dark at this time of the day, Eleanor thought as she took a deep breath and steadied herself. Thick clouds must be covering the sun. She had listened to Jake's final conversation carefully to make sure she knew the exact number of guests she should expect. It was five, counting the toddler.

She wondered if the little boy would expect a whole peach at his young age. The tin can she had opened last week had six wonderful round peaches inside. She'd felt guilty eating them all by herself, but she'd been so tired of having only beans. She regretted the impulse now. There was only one can of fruit left to serve everyone. Even if she didn't give herself one, she'd still have to cut them in half for the children. A half a peach wasn't much for Christmas dinner.

She wished she had time to write a letter to the cook at the Stout estate. Hadn't the woman poured something over peaches once and set them on fire? Eleanor had thought it was nonsense at the time, but it had been the French way of doing things and that would impress Mrs. Martin and delight the children.

Just glancing at Mrs. Martin now, though, Eleanor wondered if anything would please the older woman. Her chin was lowered as she studied a spot on the table. Eleanor figured she was bound to fail in the woman's eyes.

Instead of fretting, she walked over and put some more wood on the fireplace. She wasn't going to admit defeat and, until Christmas was over, she had nothing to say to anyone who was trying to humiliate her in hopes that Adam would see just how useless she was when it came to entertaining guests. Mrs. Martin's charge that Eleanor only knew how to talk to sheep still stung.

The irony was that she knew she wasn't the kind of wife Adam needed for the life she now saw he would be leading. If Mrs. Martin had been more polite about it, Eleanor would have gladly confessed her shortcomings. There had obviously been a misunderstanding. Even Mrs. Stout wouldn't have promoted the marriage if she had known all that Eleanor now knew. But it was too late. Christmas was coming and Adam would be embarrassed in front of his friends if she didn't do something.

Dear Lord, help me, she prayed. They had beans and those old potatoes. Would that be enough?

Would she be enough? she wondered.

She was shivering so she wrapped her arms around

herself and stood in front of the blaze for a moment. She took care not to get too close to the flame. The skirt on her pink calico dress spread fuller than the ones she usually wore. It was the best garment she owned and she'd worn it today in honor of her wedding. She knew it didn't compete with Mrs. Martin's maroon dress, and it wasn't really a bride's dress, but it was the best she had. One of the housemaids on the estate had made a lace collar for her to wear with it. She had done all she could. There was no going back.

She didn't lift her head, not even when she heard footsteps coming toward her.

"Eleanor," Adam said softly when he stood next to her.

She looked up at him and noticed the way the fire lit up his face with a golden glow. He had no right to be so handsome. His jaw line was firm and his mouth unsmiling. His hair had fine pieces of hay in it though and she almost reached up to smooth them away until she noticed the pity in his eyes.

She turned and a moment later she heard him walk away. At least no one had ever looked down on her when she had been on the Stout estate.

Then she heard his footsteps stop in front of his mother.

"Why did you do that?" he asked the older woman in a voice that betrayed no emotion, but demanded an answer.

"What?" his mother said, sounding innocent.

Eleanor looked over at the woman. She knew Adam's mother would expect a whole peach. In fact, she'd probably feel she deserved the whole peach tree. Standing there in a dress more expensive than any Eleanor could ever hope to own, the other woman casually glanced around the cabin as if she were a queen surveying an unfortunate slum that she'd been forced to visit. The tiny smile that tugged at her lips could be nothing but triumphant.

"You invited the Hargroves over for dinner," Adam said, bringing her attention back to him, his voice grim. When she didn't say anything, he opened his mouth to continue, but his mother spoke instead.

"They're your neighbors," she protested with a little self-righteous laugh. "I don't know why you're upset. You'll certainly have some civilized activities now that Hannah is here. It's a small thing to invite a family over to mark the most blessed day of the year."

"The most blessed—" Adam said incredulously and then his eyes narrowed. "God forgive you, I wish I could believe that's what you were thinking. You know we have nothing to feed them."

"Oh," his mother said, looking unsure of herself for the first time, but then she shook her head. "That can't be true. You must have something. What were you planning to feed us?"

"Beans."

"For Christmas dinner!" his mother looked truly shocked. Her voice had risen until it was louder than it had been all morning. She turned to Eleanor with real concern in her eyes.

"And we don't have many of those," Adam added before she could ask any more questions.

His mother kept shaking her head. "I don't believe it. Even out here, people must eat more than beans for Christmas dinner."

Eleanor bit back any words she might say. "It's not that easy to get supplies here. There's not a mercantile down the street."

Just then Eleanor heard a slight sound in the doorway that led to the back room. It was followed by a girlish giggle.

All three adults turned. Hannah stood there in her nightgown with her hair in disarray and a rosy smile on her face. "You're teasing me. No one has beans for Christmas. Except the bad children, but Santa brings them coal, too."

There was absolute silence. Even the sound of the blizzard outside seemed to fade.

Finally, Adam took a few steps until he stood in front of his daughter. "Hannah."

He paused and cleared his throat before squatting down and looking her in the eyes. "Honey, Christmas is about more than what kind of food we have to eat. It's a celebration no matter what is on our plates. It's the day that Jesus was born."

Adam reached out and smoothed some stray hairs away from the girl's face. She gave him a sweet smile and nodded a little uncertainly. Eleanor could see that Hannah still didn't believe there would not be something special for dinner.

"I doubt even the shepherds made do with beans," Mrs. Martin said, low enough that only Eleanor could hear. "I don't know why you couldn't do even a little bit of planning. You knew Christmas was coming."

"I did," Eleanor said. She didn't want Hannah to worry in case she could hear them. "I saved a candle."

"You what?" The other woman spoke louder than she obviously intended, her bewilderment making her forget any thoughts of being discreet. "A candle!"

"Yes. I always put a candle in the window on Christmas Eve," Eleanor said in a normal voice as she walked toward Adam and Hannah. They both looked up at her and she knelt down so she was part of their circle. She looked at Hannah. "It's something my father always used to do. And his parents before him. It's a way of honoring the Christ child."

Hannah's eyes were wistful as she stared at Eleanor. "Can I light it? I've never lit a candle."

Eleanor glanced at Adam and he nodded slightly so she continued, "I think we can make an exception for tomorrow night." She paused to get more approval and then added, "We can read the Christmas story, too, and, if the night is clear, I can take you outside and let you look through my father's telescope to see the stars. It was a star that guided the wise men to the baby Jesus."

"Really?" Hannah's eyes were wide. "I've never seen a star before."

"Of course you have," Mrs. Martin interrupted in annoyance. She walked over to where they stood and frowned down at them. "There are stars everywhere. All you have to do is go outside at night and—" The woman's voice trailed off.

Adam nodded as he put his arm around his daughter. "You probably haven't done that for a long time."

"Grandma says I need lots of sleep," Hannah said, nodding solemnly. "Because I'm sick."

It was silent again.

"You're not sick," Adam said, his words measured. "You've been injured, but that's different than being sick."

Eleanor wanted to hug the little girl, but she didn't.

"Don't tell her she's not sick," his mother said impatiently. "What do you know? I'm the one who has to hold her hand and wipe away her tears when some doctor tells her she can do something when it is clear she can't." The older woman drew in a breath. "You men don't know anything about children."

"What did the doctor say?" Adam asked, his voice sounding stern this time.

"Oh, you know how they are," his mother said, as she gave a dismissive gesture with her hands. "They don't understand how difficult it was for Hannah to be thrown from that window. Of course, she can't be expected to do what the other kids do. And those scars of hers will never go away. Just look at them."

As she said the last words, Mrs. Martin lifted the hem of Hannah's nightgown enough to show the puckered scars on her legs. "She'll never be like the other kids."

"Oh, but—" Eleanor said without thinking. She'd reacted to the look on Hannah's face. But once she'd started talking, she knew what she needed to say. She stood up and faced the older woman. "Yes, she will.

Hannah has nothing to worry about. A scar doesn't mean she's different, not in any important way."

Eleanor would have gone on to say she'd seen burned skin like that before and she knew just how well it could heal. But Adam's mother drew in her breath so sharply it sounded as if she hissed.

Then she glared at Eleanor. "You have no business—"

"Yes, she does," Adam said firmly as he stood up. "She's going to be taking care of Hannah. She'll be her mother." He paused. "And I'm the one who didn't get the supplies ordered. I sent a message, but I didn't confirm it had arrived. Under the circumstances, Eleanor behaved heroically. It was my responsibility."

"Don't be ridiculous," his mother said and then turned to look at Eleanor with undisguised hostility. "Everyone knows a wife is responsible for keeping a full larder in the house."

"I won't have you talking that way to Eleanor," Adam said, even though Eleanor knew he hadn't been able to see the glare his mother had given her.

His mother lifted her chin. "I guess I can't blame you. I was taken in by her at first, too. Although I certainly don't know why either one of us was. Anyone can see she's not much."

And with that Mrs. Martin swept into the back room, leaving the rest of them to stand there and awkwardly look at each other.

"She doesn't mean anything by her words," Adam said stiffly. "I must apologize for her. I expect the trip out here was more tiring than she realized."

Eleanor nodded. She knew better, but she didn't feel like criticizing the woman when it was obvious that Adam and Hannah both had strong ties to her. Otherwise, there would be no reason for the tears that were pooling in the girl's eyes as she stood there.

"We've all had a long trip out here," Eleanor said, forcing her voice to sound cheerful. "That's no reason for any of us to be sad, though. Christmas is coming tomorrow and we're going to have some of the best company we could possibly want."

Hannah blinked and her eyes grew wide. "Who is it?"

"Some girls who want nothing more than to meet you," Eleanor said and saw the excitement build on Hannah's face.

"What are their names?" she asked.

"The youngest one is named Mary," Adam said. "Her sister, Spotted Fawn, named her that after Christmas."

"Spotted Fawn?" Eleanor looked up in confusion. "Isn't that—"

Adam nodded. "The two girls are partly Lakota Sioux. They're Jake's nieces. They came to live with him when the fighting was so bad with the soldiers. His half brother Red Tail lived and eventually died with the Lakota people."

Eleanor was stunned. "I've never met an Indian before. Do the girls speak—" She stopped, realizing how the question might sound. Her face flushed in embarrassment. She, of all people, should know not to judge someone based on their race. Somewhere someone was probably asking if an Irish person could speak any kind of language at all.

Adam nodded with a quick glance in her direction. "The girls speak better English than I do. They go to school in Miles City. Spotted Fawn is almost finished with her studies, and I hear she's set to be a teacher next year if she can find a school to hire her. Mary is quite a bit younger. More Hannah's age."

"Do they have any dolls?" the girl asked.

Adam looked down at her. "I don't know, sweetheart. Did you bring your dolls with you?"

She shook her head. "Grandma said I should leave them in her house 'cause we didn't have any room in my trunks."

"I see," Adam said, his voice telling Eleanor he didn't approve. She wondered if he, like she, had noted the large number of hat boxes his mother had brought with her.

He didn't say anything after that.

"We'll figure out some games for you to play," Eleanor finally said. "There are lots of things you can do on Christmas."

Hannah looked at her dubiously. "I never get to play games. Grandma says there's too much shoving and running. I might get hurt."

"These will be quiet games," Eleanor assured her. "You won't need to worry."

With that, Hannah started to smile. "I can't wait for Christmas to get here."

"Me, neither," Eleanor said and gave the girl a quick hug.

"Now go get dressed," Adam said. "We have a lot to do today to get ready."

Hannah nodded as she turned and limped into the back room.

The room seemed peaceful when it was just her and Adam, she thought as she turned to him. "She's a delightful child."

He nodded. "I didn't realize my mother kept her so restricted, though."

"Your mother, she—" Eleanor said, not really knowing what she was going to say.

"Leave my mother to me," Adam said, his voice firm enough that she knew he wasn't willing to talk about it any longer. "She'll come around."

Eleanor nodded even though she knew it wasn't that simple. His mother didn't want her here and that wasn't likely to change. Seeing the tense look on Adam's face made her realize that he loved his mother despite his frustration with her. Eleanor didn't believe in splitting up families. Her parents had suffered enough with being rejected by her mother's family for her to be the one to cause strain in anyone's family.

She waited for a moment, unsure how to ask what she needed to know.

"Those letters you received," she finally asked. "The ones that answered your advertisement. Do you still have them?"

Adam frowned. "I think my mother does."

Eleanor nodded. It would be all right, then. His mother could just send for someone to replace her. She had enough money in her valise to pay her way back home to Nantucket. After Christmas, she would go. Maybe the Stouts would speak to one of their neighbors. She wasn't sure she'd have the heart to stay in this territory without Adam and his daughter.

Chapter Five

The wind had died down, but Eleanor could see by looking out the partially frosted window that the snow continued to fall steadily. It was mid-morning. After Jake's visit, they had eaten a silent breakfast of left-over beans and then Adam had gone outside to water the animals and finish unloading the wagon.

Eleanor was glad to be alone. She had slipped into the back room to get her valise while the others were eating. Now Mrs. Martin and Hannah were in the back room and she figured they were napping since the older woman had insisted Eleanor keep the kitten out while they slept. No one had said anything about the beans; they'd just sat down and eaten what she had served.

After everyone left the table, Eleanor took her valise and carefully set it beside the Christmas tree. She felt better when she had her mother's opera gloves and her father's telescope nearby.

Until now, she'd never felt poor when she had those things with her. It stiffened her resolve to know

Adam's mother would think neither one of them were worth packing across the country. But what did the woman know of life?

The opera gloves were old, Eleanor had to admit. She used to be able to smell her mother's lavender perfume when she held those gloves in her hands, even if lately when she brought them out there had been no odor. The seams had become stretched over the years and the cloth was yellowed. Eleanor still liked to hold them as she remembered the stories her parents told of the past. Her mother had worn the gloves before she met Eleanor's father, in the days when she was a carefree young woman who went to balls and concerts in Boston and New York. Those stories had become like dreams for Eleanor.

As for the telescope, it wasn't that old, but it was handmade so it would not be important in Mrs. Martin's estimation, either. Her father often told of how he'd searched for the finest piece of walnut he could find for the casing. Then he'd carved it to the shape he needed and polished it every evening for months. He'd saved a full year before sending away for the magnifying pieces he needed. Then he'd put everything together in the gardening shed of her mother's old home. The first star he'd seen, he never tired of telling her, had been the one that shone down on the rose garden where he'd first kissed her mother.

She wondered what her parents would think of the situation she was in now. They'd both been such romantics; they probably would have understood the impulse that had led her to this place in the Montana territory. Now that she knew the troubles in this small family, though, she suspected they would agree that she should leave after Christmas.

She stood there for a minute until the kitten came up and rubbed against her ankles. She bent down to pick it up.

"It's just you and me again, my friend," she whispered to the animal as she carried it over to the stool and sat down with it in her lap. She would need to write her friend from the train, Felicity Sawyer, and let her know things hadn't come to pass as she had thought they would on the banks of Dry Creek. When they went into Miles City, she would have to go to the mercantile and ask if a letter had come from Felicity.

Eleanor sat there, listening to the kitten's purr and feeling the warmth of the fire. She had not felt so alone even after her father died. The tears in Hannah's eyes earlier today made her remember the times she'd caught her mother crying. It was no small thing to be torn from the only family a girl or a young woman knew. Eleanor had always suspected that her mother had not believed her parents would so thoroughly disown her when she chose to marry a gardener.

Families should be forever, Eleanor thought. Regardless of who married who.

The temperature dropped as she sat on the stool, petting the kitten, and wondering when she should leave. Finally Eleanor got up and put more wood on the fire. There was certainly no way she could go anywhere today. And she had promised Hannah a good Christmas tomorrow.

But before she worried about the holiday, Eleanor needed to put some more beans on the back of the stove so they would have something to eat tonight. She'd left the cloth bag that held the beans on the shelf near the table and she walked over and reached up to take it down.

As she stepped to the stove, she looked at the water bucket she kept next to the wood box. It was close to the cook stove so that it wouldn't freeze over, not even at night, but it was almost empty after all of the rose hip tea she'd made this morning.

She knew people sometimes melted snow for their drinking water, but she felt better getting it from the creek. She took one last look out the window. The snow seemed to be slowing. At least she could see farther than she had been able to earlier. She should be able to go down to the creek and find her way back easily.

She might think more clearly after she'd had a brisk walk, anyway. Eleanor brought her wool scarf out of her valise and was wrapping it around her ears when the door opened and Adam stepped inside.

"I had some green coffee in my saddle bags." Adam walked over to the table and set a small leather pouch down. "Its army issue, but I expect the Hargroves are used to it. Most folks hereabouts are."

She stopped winding her scarf around her neck and stared at him. "I've never heard of green coffee."

He nodded and snowflakes fell off his hair. "It keeps longer than the roasted beans so it's what we take on patrol. Cheaper, too, since it's not dried the same. I even have some hardtack left. And, of course, your tea will be welcome. The Hargroves won't expect much."

"But they should expect something," Eleanor protested. Then—just like that—she had an idea. "I can do better."

She wasn't sure there were any fish left in the creek, but she was going to find out just as soon as she could slip away from the cabin.

"I know we'd like it to be better," Adam said patiently. "But they understand that I just got here and we haven't had time to set up our home yet. They'll be grateful for a plate of beans if it's served in friendship."

His response was so different from his mother's that Eleanor looked at him for any trace of censure in his eyes. She didn't see any, but she wasn't sure why he was being so kind about all of this. "You told me to get your house ready for Christmas. That's tomorrow. Most men would be upset that I haven't done what they had asked."

She turned around and looked, expecting him to follow her gaze. Enough light was coming in the window for him to see everything. She had meant to sew some of her flannel into a wall covering for the worst of the gray logs on the south side of the cabin, but she hadn't. She didn't know what had happened to make them look so bad.

"You won't find me being upset about that," Adam said, his voice pinched. "I'm the one who left this place the way it was."

When she didn't say anything, he continued, "Besides, everything's clean in here and you put up a tree," Adam said. "That should be good enough for anyone."

"I did knit some stars for it." Eleanor looked over at the small pine and wondered if anyone would even know what those yellow patches were. They seemed to be more twisted every day.

"Those stars are quite nice," Adam said, but she noticed he wasn't looking at her eyes when he said it.

"You don't need to spare my feelings." She squared her shoulders. "I told you I'm not very good at knitting. The points won't stay the way they should. But not many women are better or quicker than me when it comes to weaving on a loom."

"Well, see there," Adam said, his voice sounding relieved. "That's good."

"Not that I have a loom here," she reminded him. "Or any sheep for wool, either, so why would I need one?"

The challenge his mother had laid down was between the two of them, Eleanor thought as she looked at the rest of the cabin. She might have decided to leave, but that didn't mean she wanted to retreat because someone thought she couldn't do a good enough job. It wasn't the first time that Eleanor had needed to prove she was competent. Every time a new herder had come to the Nantucket area, she would have to demonstrate that she could take care of her sheep. Even though she worked for her father, the others wanted her to prove her worth as if she was an outsider.

She'd faced up to those herders. She could do the same with Mrs. Martin.

"I'm going down to the creek," she announced, as she finished looping the scarf around her head.

"It's still cold. I'll go for you," Adam said as he walked over to the water bucket.

Eleanor turned to her valise. "I just need to get some thread before I go. And we'll need the ax from the shelter."

"I already used it to cut open a space in the creek when I brought water up for the horses. I was going to go down and get another bucket filled for the house, anyway."

"We'll need that long stick that's leaning against the wall back by the hay, too," Eleanor said as she walked over and pulled the blanket off the peg by the door. "I'm going to catch us some fish."

"Fish? But I don't think—" Adam started to say, but she was already opening the door.

"I'll meet you down there," Eleanor said as she bent into the wind. "I need to see if I can find some wild onions, too. Christmas dinner should be the best we have, after all."

Adam did what he was told. He gathered the bucket and went behind the house to the shelter to get the stick. Eleanor had slipped the thread into her pocket before she left the cabin. The freezing air outside cheered him up or maybe it was the determined way Eleanor had walked out the door and faced the wind that made him feel hopeful for the years ahead. She wasn't a timid flower like his Catherine had been.

He just hoped Eleanor wouldn't be too disappointed when she didn't find anything in the creek. Some of the soldiers at the fort were fond of fishing on their days off, but he had never heard any of them boast about catching anything in these shallow creeks around here, at least not when it was this cold outside.

He smiled slightly, for some reason remembering that Jesus had multiplied the loaves and the fishes. With Eleanor's faith, he wasn't going to bet against her.

He kept walking until he topped the small rise and saw Eleanor on the banks of Dry Creek. She had squatted down, holding the blanket around her until he couldn't see anything of her but the top of her copper-colored head.

"Are you warm enough?" Adam asked when he got close.

"Yes," she whispered back, but her teeth were chattering so much he knew it wasn't completely true. "Keep your voice down and give me the pole. You'll scare the fish."

"Okay," he said quietly as he sat down on the cold ground and handed her the stick she wanted. His army coat was long and heavy so he slid close enough that he could open his coat to the side and let her settle into the warmth under his arm.

She was like ice when she leaned against him. Of course, that might be because her blanket had snow on it. Still, he sat quietly and let his body temperature adjust. Before long, he felt her shivering stop.

"It's all right if you don't catch anything," he said

after a bit. "I saw those potatoes in the shelter. We could boil them for dinner tomorrow."

"Shhhhh," she scolded him.

He smiled. A few strands of her glorious hair were blowing against his face. He was content.

The time passed and Eleanor knew she would have been forced to give up on catching anything if it weren't for the steady warm feeling of being close to Adam. She wasn't so sure it was right to let his arms encircle her when she wasn't going to stay here and marry him, but she didn't say anything. A lifetime stretched ahead of her and she suspected embraces like this would be rare when she left this place.

Still, she should tell him her decision.

Just then she felt a tug on the pole she held and bent forward in her excitement.

"I'll be," Adam said in surprise as he scrambled to his feet. "Do you need me to help pull him in?"

"Please." A glimpse through the ice showed her that the trout was larger than the other ones she'd caught here earlier and she couldn't get to her feet when the blanket was wrapped around her. She would have a hard time without help.

Adam was able to lift the fish through the hole in the ice and he laid it on the snow next to her.

"My father always said that once you catch one trout, there's another one around," Eleanor said as she removed the hook from the fish.

"My mother always said lightning never strikes in

the same place twice," Adam said with a grin as he sat back down beside her.

"Well, we'll just see who's right," Eleanor said as she put more bait on the hook and let it fall back into the freezing water.

Within the next hour, she had caught four more trout, all of them large.

"I guess your father wins," Adam said as he took the fish to string them together so they could be carried back to the cabin. "Five big ones. This is going to be some Christmas feast. You did it."

Eleanor shifted the blanket up to her shoulders as she stood up and turned to face Adam. His eyes were shining with so much approval that it made her feel shy.

"I prayed on my way down here," she confessed. "So it wasn't really me getting the fish."

"I figured as much," Adam said as he turned away and looped the string of fish around the end of the pole. "I'd say God makes a better fishing partner than most people."

"At least He knows to keep His voice down," Eleanor said, grinning up at him.

He laughed. "I guess that's true. Shall we head back?"

"I need to find some more wild onions down here, too," Eleanor said as she pointed to a snow-covered place along the river bank. "I found some over there last week."

Together they went over and scraped the snow away. The stalks were dead, but when she knelt down and pulled the plants up there were small onions on the bottoms.

"We can roast these by the fire with the fish," Eleanor said as looked over at Adam. He had knelt down beside the plants, too. Together they had gathered a couple of dozen onions and she couldn't see any more stalks. "My father used to roast them with a little bacon."

"Sounds good to me," Adam said as he stood up and brushed the snow off his knees.

Then he held out his hand to help her up and Eleanor took it. She had the onions wrapped in a corner of her blanket so she rose awkwardly and almost dropped them before she stood straight.

"Here," Adam said as he steadied her with one hand and tied a knot around the onions with the other using a corner of her blanket.

"Thank you."

She had to hold the corner of the blanket, but she still managed to look up at him. The clouds had cleared since they had started fishing and the sunlight fell bright around his head, almost making her squint. Maybe it was some stray snowflakes that made him shine so brightly, she thought. But what accounted for the warmth in his blue eyes?

"As it turns out you're even prettier in sunshine than you are in moonlight," Adam said softly.

For the first time, it occurred to her that he was courting her. She'd passed off his nonsense of last night as the effects of being tired. But she'd never had a beau before.

She knew what she should say, but she didn't have the nerve. Not when he was looking at her as if she was rare and fragile and—

The kiss surprised her even though she had known it was coming. His lips were more insistent than last night, though, and she felt her breath quicken in her throat. When he did raise his head, he still held her close enough that she could hear the beating of his heart.

"The onions," Eleanor whispered as the knot in the blanket loosened and they all fell to the snowy ground.

"I'll get them," Adam said as she started to bend down to pick them up.

She let him gather them.

It wasn't until he stepped close again so that he could tie another knot in the blanket that she found enough bravery to say the words he deserved to hear.

"I'm not staying," she said, not able to look him in the eyes. Instead, she kept her eyes focused on the top brass button on his coat. She had never realized how shiny all those buttons were. She waited for him to say something in return, but when he didn't she raised her eyes to his.

"You should go back to the house," he said indulgently. "Haven't I been telling you that all the time we've been down here? Well, all the times you would let me speak and weren't worried about me scaring away the trout."

He had the look of a satisfied man, she thought to herself, and tried not to feel pleased that kissing her could make him feel that way. "I'm not talking about here."

She should have looked away, she told herself. Instead, she saw the gradual realization that she meant something else turn his face hard.

"No," he said as he turned, and started walking up the slight hill.

Eleanor scrambled after him, balancing the pouch of onions on her hip as she went. He had the advantage of longer legs, though, and she didn't catch up with him until they were at the door to the cabin. Like the gentleman he was, he was waiting so he could open the door for her.

"You know it's not good for us to marry," she said as she stood there and he reached over to open the door.

"No, I don't know that," he said curtly as she walked into the cabin.

Eleanor was ready to give him all of the reasons why they couldn't marry. But she had only taken one step into the cabin when she heard the sobs.

"Hannah," she breathed and turned to see Adam coming right behind her.

"Where is she?" he asked.

Both of them quickly looked around the main room.

"She has to be in the back," Eleanor said as she started walking that way.

Please, Lord, she prayed as she hurried. *Don't let anything be wrong with Hannah.*

Chapter Six

There was no window in the back room but enough light filtered in through the logs and the open doorway that Eleanor could see the girl as she sat on the bed, hugging the kitten and crying as if her heart would break.

"What happened?" Adam demanded to know with a fierce glance at his mother who sat near the girl, looking bewildered.

"I didn't say anything," she protested as she lifted her finger and pointed. "It's that cat."

"The kitten?" Eleanor asked as stepped close to the bed.

She focused on Hannah and gently asked, "Did something happen?"

The girl nodded and tried to catch her breath. "Little kitty has a hurt on his leg. Just like mine."

"Oh," Eleanor said as she knelt down by the bed. She looked up at Adam and he gave her a slight nod so she kept talking. "Yes, he was hurt, but he's getting better every day. He has scars, but they're going away. Before he knows it, he'll be all well."

Hannah looked at the cat as if she wasn't sure Eleanor could be believed. "Did his mother die, too? When he was hurt? Was it a fire?"

Eleanor heard the gasps that came from both Adam and his mother, but she kept her eyes on the girl and spoke as softly as she could. "I don't know what happened to the kitten, but I think he ran in front of a wagon wheel and that's how his leg was injured."

Hannah nodded seriously. "And you're making him better? Are you a doctor?"

Eleanor shook her head. "No, but remember those sheep I used to have?"

The girl nodded.

"Sometimes they would get hurt and I had to help them get better," Eleanor said.

Hannah seemed satisfied with that and Eleanor was preparing to stand up when she heard the girl sigh.

"Can you make me better, too?" Hannah asked then, her eyes wide and her hope evident. "Like the kitty."

In her shock at being asked, Eleanor stared down at the girl's trusting eyes and was speechless.

Adam's mother shifted her position on the bed.

"Don't be ridiculous. Of course she can't." The older woman patted Hannah on the back and glared down at Eleanor. "Why, she's no more a doctor than I'm a—a—" She sputtered for a moment and then gave up. "Well, she's not a doctor. That's all there is to it."

"I only take care of lambs," Eleanor managed to add in a civil voice as she saw the hope dim in the girl's eyes.

"Was one of them your black lamb?" Hannah asked. "One of the ones that was hurt?"

Eleanor nodded. "Yes, the black lamb was one of them."

The girl was quiet for a minute. "I wish I could have seen your black lamb."

"Me, too."

"But you take care of kitties, too."

"That's right," Eleanor agreed. "Kitties, too."

With that, Hannah loosened her grip on the cat and the room seemed peaceful for a moment.

Then Adam looked down at Eleanor, "But you could treat Hannah, couldn't you? If we paid you like a doctor, could you make her better?"

"But—" His mother gasped in protest and then seemed unable to continue.

Eleanor didn't spare a glance for the other woman. Instead, she kept her eyes on Adam as he stood in the middle of the room. He was standing at attention as if he was still in the army. And he wasn't really looking at her although his eyes were turned in her direction. He was nervous, she realized suddenly. Another trait he shared with her father. Neither one of the men liked to ask for anything they desperately wanted when they thought they would be refused.

It was pride, she supposed, although she had an urge to touch his cheek with a comforting caress. He seemed so alone standing there by himself.

"It's not that simple," she said as she rose up so she'd be facing him. She took a step closer and waited until his eyes met her own. Then she had to brace herself against the pain she saw in their depths. "I'm sorry, but your mother is right. I've never used any of my salves and poultices on people. It's all been lambs and other animals. Things might be different with people."

He shut his eyes briefly and when he opened them again all of the emotion was gone from them. He had broken contact with her. "What did you use on the kitten's leg?"

She tried to convince herself it was for the best that he wanted to keep his sorrow from her. She'd only be here for a few more days.

She swallowed and waited a moment until she could answer without her voice trembling.

"I brought a salve with me that makes the skin soft around the scab," she finally said. "There's a plant leaf that I use along with some beef tallow. I use that and then I rub the leg so that the muscles are growing stronger. The kitten still limps a little, but he's starting to play again and soon he'll be able to do anything any other cat can do."

She forced herself to remember how pleased she'd been each day as she'd seen the cat improve. It had been her joy as she waited for Adam to come home. The kitten had been abandoned and was starving when she found it. She'd fed it most of the fish she'd caught in the creek and a good portion of the bacon.

Adam's mother spoke then, her fury barely contained as she faced her son. "You can't mean to have some—some animal person who isn't even a doctor pretend to treat your daughter. Why, Hannah is a delicate girl, not some old sheep out in the pasture somewhere."

"It was a lamb, Grandma," Hannah said, her voice determined as she turned to the older woman. "And a kitten."

Eleanor watched as Mrs. Martin pursed her lips together in a disapproving line.

"Maybe we should wait and talk about this—" Eleanor almost said they needed to wait until Hannah wasn't around. But she couldn't say that so she added, "Until after Christmas."

"I don't see what will be different," Mrs. Martin began, but Adam gave her a stern look and she was silent.

"That's right," Adam announced, his voice hearty. "We should wait until after Christmas because we have so much to do. Don't we, sweetheart?"

Adam was looking at Hannah and he had a smile on his face and he was crouched down with his arms open. The girl flew as fast as she could into them and said, "What, Daddy? What do we need to do?"

Eleanor felt her breath catch at the way Hannah was enclosed in Adam's hug.

"Well—" Adam kept his voice smooth, but he looked to Eleanor for help. "We could—ah—"

"We could finish decorating that tree in the other room," she offered, refusing to let any of her own longing affect her voice. She wanted to be part of that hug, but it was not to be. "And, once we finish that, we need to arrange everything for our company. And find just the right place on the window sill to set the candle tonight."

By the time Eleanor finished her list, Hannah was beaming.

"And I get to help with it all?" she asked in awe as she stepped out of her father's arms.

"Absolutely," Eleanor said and then she was caught by surprise as the girl limped over to her and hugged her tightly around her neck.

"Oh, thank you," Hannah said, her words muffled because she had her cheek pressed to Eleanor's face. "This is going to be the best Christmas ever."

Slowly, Eleanor lifted her arms to embrace the child. "Yes, I do believe you're right about that."

The embrace was over as quickly as it had begun and Hannah went to her grandmother and held out her hand. "Come. Help me with decorating the tree."

Eleanor couldn't help but notice the relief that flooded the older woman's face as she accepted her granddaughter's hand and let herself be led from the room.

"They love each other," Eleanor said as she stood up.

Adam rose, as well, and he nodded. "She's been more mother to Hannah for the past year than grandmother."

Eleanor nodded. "It will be difficult if they have to say goodbye."

Adam didn't answer that. He didn't have to. She could see by the slump in his shoulders that he knew.

She went to him then and put her hand on his arm. "It will be all right. Somehow, it will be all right."

He reached across to cover her hand with his own. "Will you pray about it for us?"

She nodded and then hesitated. "You can pray, too."

He was silent for so long that she thought he wasn't going to answer. Then he bowed his head, closed his eyes and began to pray. "Father, I need You. I've been away from You too long seeking my own forgiveness for what happened and not looking to You. I'm tired of being so far from You. We all need You. Be with us this Christmas. Amen."

Adam's eyes were damp when he opened them and gazed at Eleanor.

"Thank you for bringing me home to Him," he said as she looked up.

She swallowed and nodded. Maybe this is why God has brought her here, she thought. "What happened to Hannah and her mother wasn't your fault, you know."

Adam kept looking at her and his eyes grew tender. Then he leaned forward and kissed her.

The air in the room was cool and there was still snow in Adam's hair as she reached up to touch it. That's what made her remember—

"The fish," she gasped as she pulled away from him. "We can't leave the fish out. Not with the kitten in the room. She loves trout."

With that, they both ran, hand in hand, out into

the other room. It made Eleanor feel like a girl again, racing across the fields. She was breathless when they stopped.

Adam saw the kitten first. The little animal was cautiously approaching the table where the fish sat dripping on the floor. He recognized a hunter when he saw one, although he did see the kitten give a guilty glance in their direction.

"No," Eleanor said in a firm voice and the poor cat stopped.

"I see you caught some fish," his mother said then, her voice sounding almost disinterested. She was sitting on the stool by the fireplace with Hannah cradled on her lap.

"We need to take them out back and clean them." Eleanor took a step toward the table.

"Don't worry," Adam said. "Let me do that. You stay inside here and get warm."

Eleanor didn't say anything, but she didn't look too happy about it. Neither did his mother who looked up at those words with more interest than she'd shown in the fish.

"You were going to help Hannah decorate the tree," Adam said as he walked over and laid a hand on Eleanor's arm. He wouldn't have thought it, but she looked as if she needed courage for something.

"Yaaay," Hannah squealed as she climbed down off of his mother's lap and headed to the little pine tree in the corner. "What do I do first?"

His daughter had directed her question to Eleanor and he gave her arm an encouraging pat.

Eleanor took a deep breath and started walking to the tree herself. "Well, let me see. First we need to find some ornaments to put on its branches."

"But we don't have any ornaments."

"Maybe we do if we go looking for them."

His mother gave a dismissive snort at the notion, but Eleanor kept her gaze focused on Hannah. "The very best trees in the world are ones that are decorated with found ornaments."

"What are those?" Hannah cocked her head to the side, obviously intrigued.

"We'll know them when we find them," Eleanor said and took one of Hannah's hands. "What makes them so special is that we need to go on a hunt to find them."

"Oh." Hannah's eyes grew big. "Is it like a treasure hunt? I heard about them."

Eleanor nodded. "It's exactly like that. We'll start in the other room."

Adam watched them leave, his heart full of gratitude for how Eleanor was handling his daughter. He doubted Hannah had had much fun since the fire that changed their lives forever.

"I still have the other letters," his mother said when the two of them were alone in the room. "You don't have to marry that one. There are others. I remember one woman is a schoolteacher. She'd make a good mother for Hannah."

He turned to look at his mother. Sitting there, in the firelight, she looked tired and alone.

"It's not just for Hannah," he said softly. "I want a wife for me, too."

"You didn't seem to care before—when we made the decision about Eleanor," his mother retorted. "You didn't even want to spare the time to read the letters I sent or received from that Mrs. Stout."

"Everything's different now," he said. "I'm different."

"I don't see how," his mother said as she looked at him. "You'll never find a wife like Catherine, anyway."

He tried to keep his mouth shut, but it came out, anyway. "I certainly hope I don't." The shocked expression on his mother's face made him feel ashamed of himself. "I shouldn't have said anything. I'm sorry."

"But Catherine was perfect."

"Not for me," he said.

With that, he turned and picked up the fish on the way out of the cabin.

He was going to start a new life, he told himself, as he shut the door and turned to walk through the snow. He wasn't going to settle for gray anymore, not in his relationship with God or with other people. If Hannah was going to heal from the fire, he needed to be a man who could open his arms and love her. If he was going to be a better son, he needed to tell his mother who he was. And if he ever hoped to win the love of a woman like Eleanor, he had to be honest with himself and others.

Just then the wind blew tiny ice particles against his face. He grinned. If ice was forming that meant somewhere up in the clouds it was warm. He just needed to be patient for the warmth to come down. In a day or two they would be able to go to Miles City.

And it was going to be a good Christmas, he told himself as he carried the trout around to the shelter so he could clean them. Once the fish were ready, he would pack them in snow and put them in the back of the wagon to prevent any animals from eating them. Then he was going to go inside and show his daughter that he knew how to get ready for a holiday and show Eleanor that he was worthy to stand by her side.

Chapter Seven

The afternoon light was fading as Eleanor stood at the cook stove and stirred their evening pot of beans. Adam's mother had gone to lay down in the back room, saying she was going to take a nap. Eleanor suspected the woman just wanted to avoid being around her. Maybe if Adam was inside, the tension between her and his mother wouldn't be quite so bad, but he was out in the shelter behind the house. She could hear him moving around back there and wondered what he was doing.

When he had been in earlier, he'd asked his mother for some paper and a lead pencil. The woman had given it to him, but then cautioned him that a gentleman used ink if he was writing a letter to a lady. Her words were really a question, but he'd just grinned and said it was Christmas—a time for secrets.

Eleanor figured he was writing a letter to one of the other women who had answered his advertisement, but she refused to let it spoil her day.

Instead, she smiled down at his daughter.

"This is my favorite," Hannah said from where she stood by the small tree. She was pointing to a cluster of red wooden berries that her grandmother had taken from the brim of one of her hats and given to her for an ornament.

"It's lovely," Eleanor agreed. She'd been surprised at the generosity of the older woman when it came to making Hannah's tree pretty. Mrs. Martin had done it quietly, too, as though she often gave her granddaughter little play things.

"You're sure my daddy doesn't need his buttons?" Hannah worried as she touched one of the shiny brass circles that hung from the smallest branches. The buttons were beginning to shine in the firelight as the day began to grow dark.

"I promised I'd sew them right back on after Christmas," Eleanor said as she moved the cooked beans to the back of the stove and walked over to admire the tree again with the little girl. The pine smell had become stronger after Adam cut the end of the trunk and when one stood close to it, like she was now, the tree smelled fragrant enough to be a whole forest.

It was all quite wonderful, Eleanor told herself in an effort to be happier. She'd taken the red ribbon in her valise and, with Hannah's help, had tied a dozen small bows that they'd set on the tree branches. Then Hannah had dug through the clothes in one of her trunks until she pulled out a silver hair clip that she attached to the very top of the tree because, when it caught the light, she claimed it shone like a star.

"When can we light the candle?" Hannah asked as she looked up to where it stood on the window sill. Then she sighed in anticipation.

"We need to wait for it to get completely dark and for your father to come back inside." Eleanor had draped the black flannel from her father's telescope along the window sill and added some red ribbon for color. She was glad to see that the candle looked impressive.

"Then can we go out and see the real stars in the sky?"

"I don't know. We'll have to wait and see if the stars are out tonight," Eleanor answered.

The telescope was next to her valise, wrapped in a piece of old flannel, and the kitten was curled up next to it.

The girl seemed to think about all of that for a minute before looking up at Eleanor again.

"Grandma said I can put my daddy's present under the tree. If I hide it under the branches, he'll see it, won't he?"

Eleanor smiled. "I'm sure he'll see it the very first thing tomorrow morning."

The girl had asked her almost that exact question several times already today and each time Eleanor had assured her that Adam would not only see the present, but he would welcome it. She suspected it was something the girl had made for her father.

As for herself, she was planning to make some simple gifts after everyone went to bed. She wanted her gifts to be a surprise so she hadn't worked on them this afternoon. Besides, she needed to wait until the candle was lit before she could make her present for Hannah.

Just then Adam opened the door and came inside. She smiled when he made an elaborate show of brushing the snow off of his buttonless coat.

Hannah giggled when she saw him.

It wasn't until he took a bow that Eleanor grinned, too, understanding that he was doing it to amuse his daughter.

"I could put other buttons on your coat for today," she said when he'd stopped flapping the edges of it around. "It's no trouble."

"That's all right," he said as he finished taking the garment off. "I'm having so much fun, a little cold is nice. Tomorrow is coming fast."

With that, he went over to the fireplace and held his hands out to the warmth of the flame. "It should be warming up out there. There's some hail so maybe tomorrow will be better."

"Do you think the clouds will go away?" Eleanor asked as she walked over to where he stood. "Hannah has been asking about looking at the stars tonight."

"I don't think the sky will be clear by then," Adam said.

Then he looked at Eleanor, his eyes warm with faith and confidence. "Maybe Christmas night will be better. Maybe everything will be better by then."

"Did you write a letter?" she asked with her throat tight. She hadn't meant to ask, but how could she not?

"No." He looked up in surprise and then seemed to understand. "I'm never writing that letter."

With that, he opened his arms and Eleanor found herself sliding into his embrace as though it was the natural thing to do. His shirt was cold as she laid her cheek against it. He wrapped his arms around her tight and they just stood there.

"Christmas is a time of hope, after all," he said softly as he moved far enough away to brush the hair away from her face. "I'm not giving you up."

Eleanor looked at his eyes, memorizing them for her dreams. "But your mother—"

"I'm not giving you up," he repeated. "That's all I know."

Finally, Hannah's voice came to them. "Is it dark yet? Can we light the candle?"

Eleanor turned to see the little girl looking at them impatiently.

"Let's eat first, shall we?" she said as she started to walk toward the table. "Then we'll light the candle after we read the Christmas story. Just before you go to bed."

Hannah nodded.

"That way you'll have Christmas dreams," Eleanor turned to say to the girl.

With Hannah's encouragement, their supper was over and they were gathered in front of the fire before much time had passed. Adam's mother sat on the stool and everyone else sat on the buffalo robe. Adam had brought in plenty of wood and stacked it high so the flame would give off enough light for him to read from the Bible.

As Adam read the holy words, he stopped at the first mention of shepherds and looked over at Eleanor with a smile.

His mother cleared her throat before Eleanor could say anything in response.

"We know," the older woman said impatiently. "The sheep were good enough for God. You don't have to tell us."

"But I didn't mean—" Adam turned to his mother in startled distress.

Eleanor thought the other woman looked tired and discouraged.

"Just read the story," his mother snapped.

And so he did. Hannah's face lit up at the mention of the star that had guided the wise men. And Eleanor smiled when they wrapped the baby in swaddling clothes.

"I never realized what ordinary people Mary and Joseph were," Adam said as he finally closed the Bible. They were quiet together for a while after that, each watching the fire and remembering what had happened thousands of years ago.

Finally, Eleanor reached over for the long twig she'd taken out of the wood box earlier so that Hannah would be able to light the candle in the window.

Adam lifted his daughter up and Eleanor handed the girl the smoldering twig.

"Careful now," she said as Hannah held the twig out to light the candle that was balanced on the sill. The night was dark outside but tiny flakes of snow flew past the window.

When the girl drew the twig back slightly, Eleanor stepped forward and took it so she could blow it out.

Adam's mother walked over and stood next to them as they watched the candle burn.

"Peace on earth and good will to men," Eleanor muttered after a bit.

Then Adam suggested they form a circle and pray together. The wind outside had grown worse and a shiver ran down Eleanor's back as she reached out her hands to Adam and Hannah. She had one more day to be in this family circle, she thought as she bowed her head. And then she didn't know what God had for her.

"We're grateful for the birth of Your Son, Lord," Adam prayed, his head bowed and his voice reverent. "It's a mystery to me that You would give Your Son to make us your family, but we're grateful all the same. Keep us mindful of Your love for us. Amen."

Adam's mother and daughter went to the back room to get ready for bed, but Adam stood with Eleanor watching the embers of the fire.

"My mother will come around," he said after a minute. "She might be difficult, but she loves me and Hannah."

"I know," Eleanor said, wishing it wasn't so. If his mother was cold toward her son and granddaughter, the choice would not be difficult. Eleanor would stay. But how could she marry Adam if it meant his family was broken apart?

Fortunately, he did not ask her to make a choice. He

might not even realize there was a choice. Instead, he wrapped her in his arms again briefly before saying he needed to finish his work in the shelter and that he'd see her in the morning.

Eleanor didn't want him to leave, but nodded, anyway. It would take her hours to do what she needed to do for tomorrow, as well.

Adam glanced back at Eleanor before he opened the door. He didn't like leaving her alone, not when she stood there in the firelight with her copper hair shining and her eyes dark with sadness.

"We need to have faith," he whispered across the room.

She nodded, but did not hold his gaze for long.

"I'll see you in a few hours," he added.

"Christmas morning," she said with a smile. "Hannah will be up early."

With that, he opened the door and faced the storm outside. Gradually, his eyes adjusted to the dark and he could see enough to follow the walls of the house until he found the door to the shelter. He had carried the presents he'd bought in Miles City into the shelter this afternoon.

In anticipation of meeting Eleanor, he'd brought a hat that his mother had selected from those on display at a small shop on the edge of town. He'd known all day that the hat was not something Eleanor would like so he'd decided to give it to his mother along with the brooch he'd picked out for her when he first heard she was coming.

Hannah's gift was a new gray coat with a black velvet collar. He'd sent away for it months ago.

Once he had decided not to give the hat to Eleanor, he'd sat down and thought about what he could give her instead. He had a few finishing touches to add to her gift, but since it was dark, he'd have to complete it in the morning. Hopefully, the horses would be co-operative then so he could continue to use them as his guide.

Adam settled down in the hay even though he could still hear movements on the other side of the fire-place. Eleanor was up, watching over the fire again. He could not remember the last time Christmas had much meaning for him. But thinking of her and all she had done to make the holiday joyous for his daughter almost overwhelmed him. He knew she was restless and not settled in his family yet, but the time had to come.

We need her, Lord, he prayed. *Help her to know she belongs here with us.*

Chapter Eight

Eleanor woke slowly, realizing the wind had died down. The fire was almost out and there was barely enough light in the room to see the walls and furniture. She'd fallen asleep late last night on the buffalo robe, but the new day already showed promise. A faint pink glow in the window meant the sun was struggling to come up. The storm was over.

It was Christmas morning and, as she lay there, she heard a rustling in the other room.

She scarcely had time to slip the presents she'd made last night under her blanket before the sound of little feet made her look up to see Hannah peek around the curtain.

"She's awake," the girl turned to whisper to her grandmother who was still in the back room. "Can I go out now?"

Eleanor heard a mumbled answer, which must have been yes since Hannah came into the room, her face alive with excitement.

"Merry Christmas," Eleanor whispered as she sat up and opened her arms.

The little girl hurried to her for a hug.

Eleanor didn't want to let go when she held the child. But Hannah had other things on her mind.

"Are there presents?" the girl asked as she studied the tree, trying to see the shapes around it in the dim light.

"We have to wait for your father and your grandmother," Eleanor insisted. "Let's go over and sit at the table and I'll make you a cup of my Christmas tea."

"You have Christmas tea?" she squealed. "Is it for little girls, too?"

"It's especially for them," Eleanor said as she stood up and smoothed back her hair. Fortunately, she'd slept in one of her wool dresses so she could leave the blanket on the buffalo robe to cover the presents.

Hannah got the tin cups down from the lowest shelf while Eleanor put some water into the kettle. She'd thought of the tea last night and taken what she needed out of her valise so she had enough dried spices to make the fragrant drink she remembered serving to her father last winter. With a few drops of the peppermint oil, it would taste festive enough to be served in the finest establishment on the East Coast. She would taste it first, though, just to be sure the peppermint mixed well. She wanted to avoid any criticisms Adam's mother might make today.

A knock on the shelter side of the fireplace let them know Adam was awake. Hannah rushed over and knocked back so he'd know to come join them.

While the girl rushed to invite her grandmother to have tea with them, Eleanor was able to slip her presents beneath the tree. She hadn't been able to wrap them and her gift for Adam was only partially completed.

It took a few minutes for everyone to gather and sit at the table, but in that short time the sun rose more fully and the shadows in the cabin gave way to daylight. Before long, the whole cabin smelled of peppermint and spice.

At the table, Eleanor and Hannah shared a trunk for seating. Adam's mother had the stool and he sat on the other trunk.

"Wonderful tea," Adam said after a long sip.

"Thank you," Eleanor said. She'd managed to not only taste the tea, but to slip into the back room and change into another dress before Adam came over. She'd saved a red ribbon to wear around her neck and it made even the gray flannel look festive.

"Isn't the tea wonderful, Mother?" Adam asked.

"She doesn't need to—" Eleanor began, but the older woman interrupted.

"Yes, of course. No one ever said the woman couldn't make a decent cup of tea."

Eleanor hid a smile. She rather thought that had been implied in the general criticisms the other woman had made of her skills as a hostess. But she didn't want to hold a grudge. "Thank you."

No one had any appetite for cold beans, not when they were going to have a meal of roasted trout and bacon-fried onions in a few hours, so they lingered over their tea. Adam was the first one to suggest they sing a Christmas hymn, but then Eleanor had a few favorites, too. Even Mrs. Martin asked them to sing 'Silent Night.'"

Finally, it was time to open the presents. They moved back to the fireplace, with Adam's mother on the stool, and the rest of them sitting on the buffalo robe.

"We'll take turns giving out the gifts," Adam said once they were all comfortable. "Hannah you can be first to pass the presents you're giving."

The girl sprang up from where she was sitting and walked as fast as she could. She'd put her gifts behind the tree and knew exactly where they were. She pulled out three packages wrapped in brown paper.

Eleanor was proud of the girl as she gave her father the present she'd made for him. Adam opened it and thanked her in genuine delight as he looked at the handkerchief she'd embroidered with his initials. He passed the cloth to Eleanor so she could see it, as well.

"Very nice," she complimented the beaming girl. "I know grown women who don't have as fine a hand at embroidery as you do."

The girl then produced two ladies handkerchiefs, one for her grandmother and one for Eleanor.

"I made them before I came," the girl confessed as she sat back down close to her father. "Grandma said I should make them with your married initials."

"Well, they are perfect," Eleanor said. "You did such a nice job on the *E* and the *M*."

Adam's mother was next and she went into the back room and brought out two hat boxes.

"They weren't all filled with my hats." The woman smiled as she gave one of the boxes to her son and the other to Hannah. "I just figured no one cared enough about hats to be curious and look inside them."

Adam opened his box and found a white Stetson.

"For when you're an important cattle rancher," the woman said to him. "Why, you might even end up in politics. Governor, even. Wouldn't that be something fine?"

"Thank you, Mother," Adam said politely. "I'll keep it for church."

Eleanor knew white would not wear well around here, but it was a handsome hat. There was no time to voice her admiration for the gift though because Hannah had opened her box.

"Ohhhhh," the girl screamed as she reached in and pulled out a beautiful china doll with long blond ringlets and a blue silk dress. Hannah looked up at her grandmother. "She's for me? I've never seen such a pretty doll."

"Of course it's for you. Come give me a hug, then," her grandmother suggested in an indulgent voice.

Hannah did just that, holding on to the older woman long enough to make tears form in the woman's eyes.

"And now it's Eleanor's turn," Adam said.

She nodded shyly and stood to walk over to the tree. Her handmade gifts didn't seem so grand when compared to the ones Mrs. Martin had given. But they came from her heart, she told herself.

She hadn't had paper or a box to wrap her gifts, so she folded her skirt around the one for Hannah as she walked over to where the little girl sat on the older woman's lap.

"This is for you, Hannah," she said as she brought the gift out and held it out to the girl.

"Ohhh." Hannah set her doll down on her grandmother's lap and reached for the black stuffed lamb Eleanor had hand-stitched for her last night. "For me?"

The girl clutched the lamb to her chest, and now the tears were in her eyes. "I've never had a lamb before. Thank you."

"You're welcome," Eleanor said.

Just then a horse neighed and some bells rang nearby.

"That must be the Hargroves," Jake said as he stood up.

"The girls?" Hannah asked although no one had time to answer because there was a knock at the door and, before anyone could think, the small cabin was bursting with Christmas greetings.

"My wife wanted us to come in caroling," Jake said, as he stood grinning in the doorway with his family behind him.

"Come in. Come in," Eleanor invited them.

"Of course, we couldn't agree on which song to sing so we thought we'd wait and get warm first." As Adam spoke he stepped to the side and, a pleasant-faced woman and toddler entered, followed by two brown-skinned girls, with their shiny black hair pulled back into long center braids and their brown eyes bright with eagerness.

"My word," Adam's mother gasped loudly. She stood up from the stool and gawked at them. "They're Indians."

Everything went silent. Even the cat stopped walking across the floor.

"I'm—I'm sorry," Adam finally breathed out as his stricken eyes sought out those of his guests. "I forgot to mention anything to my mother. That is, she's from back East and—"

Jake and his wife looked around the cabin cautiously.

"We've been so excited that you were coming," Eleanor rushed to say as she took a step toward the family in the doorway. "Please come in. You must be cold. I've made some of my special Christmas tea and I can't wait for all of you to taste it."

She was talking too fast. She knew that. But no one moved.

"Please," Eleanor said again as she slowed her voice and opened her hand, hoping the gesture would show them they were indeed welcome.

Jake's wife looked at her husband for a second, and then took a step into the cabin.

She met Eleanor's eyes. "Jake told me you knew how to make wonderful teas. Coffee is so expensive we don't often have it so I was hoping you could tell me what you use."

"I would be delighted." Eleanor led the Hargroves over to the table.

"Here, sit on the trunks," she said as everyone gathered around the table.

Jake dug into a cloth bag he'd been carrying over his shoulder and produced six tin cups, one after another. "I noticed you weren't set up for housekeeping yet so we brought a few things with us."

"Thank you," Eleanor said.

It wasn't until she started placing all of the cups around that she noticed Adam's mother had left. She must have gone into the back room.

For the next few hours, laughter and good will filled the small cabin.

Finally, Adam looked around. The smell of the trout mingled with the aroma from the wild onions. They both mixed with the smell of the peppermint tea that they had all declared to be the best Christmas drink ever made.

Hannah and the two girls were giggling in the corner, making up stories about the adventures of that black lamb and petting the kitten when he got jealous and meowed for attention. The porcelain doll his mother had given Hannah was lying forgotten in front of the Christmas tree.

Adam had tried to apologize for his mother, but Jake refused to hear it, saying he was not responsible for anyone else's prejudices. So he didn't mention it again. He had gone into the back room several times to ask his mother to come out, but she had refused.

Even with that difficulty, the day was more satisfying than any he'd had in years. Eleanor and Jake's wife were sitting at the table and, from the words he could hear, they were talking about what could be used around here to dye wool. Jake had spoken about the cattle coming up from Texas in a few months and he'd quietly told him about the gift he had for Eleanor. The other man had nodded and said he approved and could be of some help.

"This has been a good Christmas," Adam said when he pulled his attention back to his friend. "Thanks for bringing Eleanor home from the train station."

"We need wives like her here," the other man said as he patted his stomach. "That's the best trout I've had in a long time. I'm planning on you inviting us to the wedding."

"If there is a wedding," Adam said with a look over at Eleanor. "I'm not sure she will agree to take me with the way my mother is acting toward her."

Jake nodded at that. "That could be a problem. I'll pray for all of you."

"Please," Adam said.

Soon after that the sun started to go down and Jake called to his family, saying it was time for them to leave.

The cabin felt empty when they were gone.

Then Eleanor looked over at the cook stove.

"I didn't make any beans for supper," she said, almost in surprise.

"I'll go around back and get the rest of the potatoes," Jake said. "We can fry them up with the leftover onions. That'll be fine."

"I saved a piece of the trout for your mother," Eleanor said as she lifted a lid on the skillet. "I hope she's feeling better now."

Adam started to correct her.

But he saw by the look in Eleanor's eyes that she wasn't going to force his mother to acknowledge her rudeness to their guests. And when she went over to the curtains and talked with his mother, inviting her to come have something to eat, she did it in a respectful voice that told him the incident would not be mentioned unless his mother brought it up.

He couldn't fault Eleanor for showing his mother more courtesy than she deserved. He only nodded, though when his mother left the table after she had eaten, saying she was going to lie down.

"We haven't got all the presents yet, though." Hannah spoke up before his mother reached the doorway. "Aren't you going to see what's left?"

"You look for me, child," his mother said, her voice more kind than it had been all day. Then she went into the back room.

Hannah went over to stand by the tree waiting for everyone else to come.

"We got interrupted when you were giving out your gifts," Adam said to Eleanor when the three of them were sitting around the tree. "Are there more?"

Eleanor nodded shyly. "I have something for your mother. Just a handkerchief, but it has lace around it that's nice. I'll give it to her later."

Then she reached under the branches to pull out something covered with a large white handkerchief.

"This isn't finished so it's more of a promise than a gift."

With that, she passed what she had in her hands to him.

He removed the handkerchief and saw a ball of beautiful black yarn with her knitting needles sticking out of it and a dozen or so rows of yarn already knit.

"It's going to be a scarf for around your neck," she said. "It's the best yarn that I have. It's pure so it'll never fade. I collected from the black sheep for several years to get enough."

"I've never seen anything like it," Adam said as he held the two inches up that she had managed to knit. "It looks like the night sky."

The yarn shined until he thought he could see stars in the blackness.

"What else?" Hannah demanded as she came over and leaned against him.

"You're wondering what I got you?" he asked with a grin.

His daughter nodded.

"Your gift is hanging on a peg in the back room," he said. "I put it there earlier today when you were out here."

With that Hannah rushed to the other room.

"She's excited," Eleanor said as she watched the girl open the curtains and squeal.

"I wanted to give you your present while she's not around, anyway," Adam said as he moved over closer to Eleanor and handed up a rolled piece of paper.

"For me?" Eleanor said with what he thought was some trepidation.

He nodded as he kept holding it out to her.

She accepted it finally and unrolled the paper.

"What?" she gasped as she saw his drawing.

"I couldn't get them right," he said. "I tried to use the horses as examples, but they're too large and—"

"They're sheep," Eleanor said, her face vulnerable in its longing.

"How could you tell?"

She smiled, blinking her eyes. "It was the black one in the middle."

"I knew he was your favorite so I figure we can get some of them as lambs this spring. Jake said he'd help me find what I need to buy. He knows a man who has sheep down south of here a few hundred miles—black and white."

"But—"

He winced, knowing what was coming.

"They're yours whether you decide to stay or not. If you go back East, I'll see that you have your own flock there."

Her tears started in earnest then, and he opened his arm to pull her close to his side.

They sat that way for a minute until Hannah came out of the back room, wearing her new coat.

"Daddy, Daddy," she called when she got close enough to see Eleanor's tears. "Your new handkerchief. Use your handkerchief."

Adam started to chuckle as he pulled his Christmas gift out of his pocket and offered it to Eleanor with a gallant nod of his head. That made Eleanor laugh a little, as well. Which made Hannah giggle. And soon they were all three rolled up on the floor in a joyous tangle of Christmas merriment.

He didn't hear his mother come into the room until she was standing almost on top of them.

"Whatever is going on?" Her voice indignant. "I thought someone was hurt with all of this noise."

Adam wiped the tears of laughter from his eyes. "No, Mother, we're all fine."

"I see that," his mother said.

There was no longer any censure in her voice. She seemed tired and confused. All of the laughter left his heart. Something was wrong.

"I give up," his mother said then. She turned to look at Eleanor. "I have never seen my son laugh. Not like this. It seems you can make him happy in a way— well, I'll be leaving tomorrow on the train if you will be so kind as to take me to the station."

With that, his mother walked slowly to the other room. And he just sat there.

Hannah stared at where her grandmother had been.

"You can't let her go tomorrow," Eleanor whispered to him as she stood up. "Not like this. I'm going to go talk to her."

"Not alone, you're not."

"Yes, just me," Eleanor said softly as she began to walk to the back room.

The room was cold and Eleanor hesitated at the doorway. Enough light was coming through the cracks that she could see the older woman as she lay on the bed. The woman didn't turn to look at her as she stepped into the room.

"I—" Eleanor began.

"Did you come here to gloat?" the older woman asked as she finally turned to face her.

"Of course not."

"Well, it wouldn't surprise me if you did. You won."

"What exactly did I win?" Eleanor said with some anger now. "We're not talking about some game here. This is your son and granddaughter."

"I know who they are," the woman responded fiercely as she swung her legs around and stood up. "I've raised them both."

"And they love you for it."

Eleanor watched as the woman's steps faltered and her shoulders slumped. "Do you think so?" Then she looked at Eleanor fully. "I honestly have never seen them happier."

"So why are you leaving like this, then? There's no need to go so soon."

Adam's mother looked astonished. "But I treated you horribly."

"Yes," Eleanor said as she stepped close enough to the older woman to put her arm around her, "and I plan on forgiving you for all of it if you'll give me away at my wedding."

"Me?"

"You're the one who brought Adam and me together," Eleanor said with a smile. "You picked me out of all the letters you received."

It was silent for a moment.

"I did, didn't I?" the older woman finally said.

Eleanor nodded as she started walking with her arm around Mrs. Martin.

Hannah and Adam sat on the floor staring as the two women came into the main room.

"Your mother is going to give me away," Eleanor announced and then, lest there be any confusion, "At our wedding." And then she looked at Adam. "If you still want—"

Hannah started to squeal and Adam stood up only to walk over to Eleanor and drop down on one knee. "I love you, Eleanor Hamilton McBride. Will you be my wife?"

Eleanor nodded, "I'd love to, but my name—"

"I know. It's only McBride, but someday maybe we'll see about uniting your family, too."

With that Adam stood and opened his arms to embrace her. She was the one to reach out to draw his mother into the circle. Hannah, clutching her lamb, was already beside her father so the four of them came together.

"Oh," Adam's mother said once the circle was complete, her voice filled with delight and hope.

Then she grabbed Hannah's hand and suggested they go to bed early.

Adam and Eleanor sat by the fireplace for the next hour, talking about their dreams for their life together. Then, seeing how clear the sky was, they called Hannah from her bed and took her outside to see the Christmas stars that were sparkling in the night sky.

* * *

The next morning was clear and the sun was shining. The snow on the ground was melting slightly when Adam came in the cabin, saying he was going to ride over and tell the Hargroves to meet them at the church in Miles City while the women got dressed.

"I can't wait until we have our own church out here," Adam said before he left. "And a school. Jake says enough families are settling around here that we'll have a community before we know it."

Eleanor changed into her pink calico dress after he left and tried to tame her curls enough to make her hair look dignified.

"Here, let me," Mrs. Martin finally said and managed to make her hair respectable for the day.

"Thank you," Eleanor said.

The other woman waved her words away. "I have something for you, too. Let me get it."

She came back with a strand of white pearls, unclasping them and putting them around Eleanor's neck.

"My mother gave me those pearls," she said. "I'd like to give them to you for a wedding present. The only request I make is that you give them to Hannah on her wedding day, too."

Eleanor blinked back her tears. "I don't know what to say."

"Say we're family," the older woman said brusquely. "And don't cry all over that pretty dress of yours."

"Yes, Mother," Eleanor said and watched the other woman as a slow smile spread over her face.

The ride into Miles City was shorter than Eleanor remembered it being when she went the opposite direction that day she had stepped off the train. Adam kept whistling, and Eleanor found herself humming along.

They stopped at the mercantile when they first drove into Miles City because Adam said the storekeeper would need time to get their order together. Eleanor was pleased to be given a letter from her friend Felicity.

"See, she is alive," Eleanor told everyone once they were back on the wagon. "The woman I met on the railroad coming out here."

"Well, what does she say?" Adam's mother asked.

Eleanor opened the letter and read it quickly. "All is well. I need to write her back and tell her that Adam and I are getting married."

"Well, of course you are," the older woman said. "That's why you came out here, isn't it?"

Adam chuckled at that and Eleanor joined in. Then, right there in the middle of the street of Miles City, he stopped the wagon and turned to brush a kiss across her lips.

A cheer went up from a group of people waiting on the porch of the church and Eleanor looked over to see the Hargroves standing in front of several men, women and children.

"There's our wedding party," Adam said as he started the horses moving again.

"Hey, aren't you supposed to wait and kiss the bride

after the ceremony?" one of the men shouted from the church.

Adam chuckled and yelled back, "I plan to kiss her every chance I get."

And, to prove his point, he leaned toward her again.

Eleanor barely had sense enough after that kiss to wonder if she should recommend this mail-order business to some of her friends back East. Love happened in wonderful ways when it started with a letter.

* * * * *

Dear Reader,

I can practically see the candle in the window that shone out into the night. Few people in the Montana territory had many possessions, but almost everyone had at least that much to mark the day.

I am a big fan of traditions at Christmas, whether it's a well-placed candle or an evening of caroling. This Christmas, I hope you will find a way to honor His birth that makes you feel closer to others. I always look forward to a Christmas Eve church service and would recommend you find one in your area. And then, afterward, stand and look at the sky for a few minutes, wondering what it would have been like for the wise men to follow a star that was leading them to Jesus.

If you have a minute, I would love to hear from you. Just go to my website at www.janettronstad.com and email me from there. May you have a blessed Christmas this year.

Sincerely,

Janet Tronstad

Questions for Discussion

1. Eleanor McBride went West to marry a man she did not know because her father had died and her future was uncertain. Have you ever been in a situation where you have reached for something that was a little scary because you felt you had no choice? What happened?

2. One of Eleanor's most precious possessions was the telescope that belonged to her father. What do you think that telescope says about her relationship with her father? Do you have something that represents a close relationship in your life?

3. I have often wondered how difficult it would be to homestead in the West. But, in truth, we all face new challenges in our lives—things we feel unprepared to face. What are some of those things in your life?

4. Because Eleanor was Irish, she saved a candle to put in the window on Christmas Eve. Do you have any Christmas traditions related to your heritage? What are they?

5. Adam Martin's faith was dormant. It was there, but so weak he scarcely thought of God. What caused this for Adam? Have you ever found yourself in the same situation? What scripture verses

would you recommend to someone who felt God had abandoned them?

6. Adam's mother was so certain she knew what was best for Adam and his daughter, that she almost alienated them. What scripture verses would you suggest for her if she asked for some guidance?

INSPIRATIONAL

Wholesome romances that touch the heart and soul.

Love Inspired.
HISTORICAL

COMING NEXT MONTH
AVAILABLE JANUARY 10, 2012

THE COWBOY TUTOR
Three Brides for Three Cowboys
Linda Ford

AN INCONVENIENT MATCH
Janet Dean

ALL ROADS LEAD HOME
Christine Johnson

THE UNLIKELY WIFE
Debra Ullrick

REQUEST YOUR FREE BOOKS!

2 FREE INSPIRATIONAL NOVELS
PLUS 2
FREE
MYSTERY GIFTS

Love Inspired
HISTORICAL
INSPIRATIONAL HISTORICAL ROMANCE

YES! Please send me 2 FREE Love Inspired® Historical novels and my 2 FREE mystery gifts (gifts are worth about $10). After receiving them, if I don't wish to receive any more books, I can return the shipping statement marked "cancel". If I don't cancel, I will receive 4 brand-new novels every month and be billed just $4.49 per book in the U.S. or $4.99 per book in Canada. That's a saving of at least 22% off the cover price. It's quite a bargain! Shipping and handling is just 50¢ per book in the U.S. and 75¢ per book in Canada.* I understand that accepting the 2 free books and gifts places me under no obligation to buy anything. I can always return a shipment and cancel at any time. Even if I never buy another book, the two free books and gifts are mine to keep forever.

102/302 IDN FEHF

Name _____ (PLEASE PRINT)

Address _____ Apt. #

City _____ State/Prov. _____ Zip/Postal Code

Signature (If under 18, a parent or guardian must sign)

Mail to the **Reader Service:**
IN U.S.A.: P.O. Box 1867, Buffalo, NY 14240-1867
IN CANADA: P.O. Box 609, Fort Erie, Ontario L2A 5X3

Not valid for current subscribers to Love Inspired Historical books.

Want to try two free books from another series?
Call 1-800-873-8635 or visit www.ReaderService.com.

* Terms and prices subject to change without notice. Prices do not include applicable taxes. Sales tax applicable in N.Y. Canadian residents will be charged applicable taxes. Offer not valid in Quebec. This offer is limited to one order per household. All orders subject to credit approval. Credit or debit balances in a customer's account(s) may be offset by any other outstanding balance owed by or to the customer. Please allow 4 to 6 weeks for delivery. Offer available while quantities last.

Your Privacy—The Reader Service is committed to protecting your privacy. Our Privacy Policy is available online at www.ReaderService.com or upon request from the Reader Service.

We make a portion of our mailing list available to reputable third parties that offer products we believe may interest you. If you prefer that we not exchange your name with third parties, or if you wish to clarify or modify your communication preferences, please visit us at www.ReaderService.com/consumerschoice or write to us at Reader Service Preference Service, P.O. Box 9062, Buffalo, NY 14269. Include your complete name and address.

LIH11B

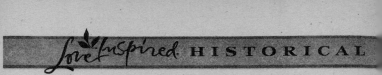

Love Inspired HISTORICAL

Introducing a brand-new trilogy
from bestselling author

Linda Ford